THE
DISTANCE
BETWEEN
US

A Hidden-Identity Romance

ANNE TROWBRIDGE

THE DISTANCE BETWEEN US

A Hidden-Identity Romance

ANNE TROWBRIDGE

Cruz Into Love Series: Book 1

© 2024 Anne Garcia

This is a work of fiction. All of the characters, organizations, and events portrayed in this novel are either products of the author's imagination or are used fictitiously.

ISBN: 979-8-9865072-5-5

For my son, Alexander.

*You're confident, smart, funny,
and always, always kind.*

*Keep that competitive spirit of yours,
but also that loving heart.*

Other Books by Anne Trowbridge

Cruz Into Love Series

The Distance Between Us:
A Hidden-Identity Romance (Book 1)
(also available now in Kindle Vella)

The Friendship Divide:
A Friends-to-Lovers Romance (Book 2)
(coming soon, but available now in Kindle Vella)

What Separates Us:
An Enemies-to-Lovers Romance (Book 3)
(coming soon, but available now in Kindle Vella)

The Curveball Incident Series

Curveball: A Love Story (Book 1)

Curveball: A Wedding Novella (Book 1.5)

Out of the Park: A Romance (Book 2)

Thrown: A Baseball Romance (Book 3)
(coming soon, but available now in Kindle Vella)

Ticket to Love Series

The Honeymoon: A Second-Chance Romance (Book 1)
(also available now in Kindle Vella)

The Bridesmaid: An Insta-Love Romance (Book 2)
(also available now in Kindle Vella)

Chapter 1

The Light Dims

I NOTICED the exact moment it happened, the agonizing instant the light in her face disappeared behind dark clouds of sadness.

I knew precisely when it happened because I'm observant like that. Plus…well, okay, it was mostly because I've been lurking around and crushing on Lily like a starstruck fanboy ever since she moved into the apartment next to mine almost a year ago. I know all her usual expressions now. Although, to be totally honest, her typical look is whatever expression says "bubbly." Like she was created in a cheerfulness lab and came preset with all the default factory settings. She's…okay, I know this is super corny, but she's *sunshine.* Her rays pull me in like nothing I've ever experienced before, because if she's sunshine…I don't know…but I think maybe I'm an eclipse.

It happened immediately for me, that sizzle of awareness and attraction, and I hadn't even seen her gorgeous face yet. I was instantly on high alert from the day she moved in just from the sound of her sweet voice. I was home working—because I don't really go anywhere else—when I heard the banging noises and the grunts and strains of her friends and family as they lifted her furniture and thumped her boxes and knickknacks into those small rooms. The walls are thin enough that I knew right away the new tenant had arrived. But that wasn't what caught my attention. After

"

all, I hadn't exactly been enthralled by the previous one, whose name may or may not have been Gus. The most interaction we ever had was me sometimes cautiously waving hello and him reluctantly nodding back.

But Lily's moving day? *That* I noticed. Her infectious happiness can seep right through the walls, apparently, because I heard the silver peals of her laughter and the musical lilt of her chatter, and that was it. I was hooked. Because of *course* she could make even moving into a dumpy apartment sound like eating an ice cream cone on a summer day at a carnival. And, honestly, from that day on, I've been utterly jealous of anyone lucky enough to be on the other side of that wall—and on the receiving end of one of those precious smiles.

Even if we weren't neighbors, I still would have noticed her. She's so consistently *up,* no matter what boring stuff she's doing. Checking the mail? She'll laugh and chat with anyone who happens to be in the lobby. Separating her whites and colors in the laundry room? She's joking with the janitor, who knows her by name—because of course he does—or any of the other tenants who happen to be nearby. She's optimistic, radiant, and outgoing—basically everything I'm not. I guess that's why I can't get her out of my head. Opposites attracting and all that. I'm the weary wanderer dying of thirst in the desert, and Lily is the crystal glass of refreshing, ice-cold water. And that potentially lifesaving drink is, ultimately, out of my reach.

That's the problem right there. Despite being my neighbor, Lily isn't within my reach. No, not me. Not good old, socially shutdown Max. I'm basically locked in a jail of shyness and anxiety, and I have been since…well, always. But especially since high school. Those years, for me, were like trying to walk into the ocean. You want nothing more than to get your feet under you and find your balance, but meanwhile waves of fear and condemnation are constantly trying to pull you down and sweep you away.

It wasn't even a typical high school thing like you see in the movies. I wasn't unlucky enough to get labeled or lumped in with a group of dorks. I wasn't a band geek or a nerd or a burnout or a gearhead. I was just so lost inside myself that I'm pretty sure no one even knew I'd been there at all. I was like furniture or wallpaper; part of the setting where the action of everyone else's lives took place. I barely registered on any of my classmates'—or teachers'—minds. They didn't talk to me, and I definitely didn't talk to them. I mean, don't get me wrong: I'm glad I don't have a sadsack backstory of being shoved into lockers or wedgied in the middle of the basketball court during homecoming. But to not even be *noticed?* That's a different kind of suffering altogether. So, yeah, I didn't make any waves, but I definitely didn't make any friends, either. I'll bet if you pointed to my picture in the yearbook, most of my former classmates would wonder if I had been included as some kind of a printing error.

After I graduated, as much as I wanted my college degree, I just couldn't force myself to navigate campus life. Dorms? Student organizations and activities? I had managed to bellycrawl through high school, but to keep going in that environment? I just…I couldn't do it. Almost no one in my family was surprised, and I guess they didn't think I could do it, either, because I didn't get a whole lot of pushback. One apartment and one online degree later, and, well...let's just say I've never really faced any of my social challenges head on.

You know what the really crazy part is? I could do okay with women now, looks-wise anyway, if I could just move past all the things that paralyze me and make me want to remain invisible. Here's an irony for you: My brother Jake is a personal trainer and a model. Actually, both my brothers are. They're twins. Mitch and Jake are almost completely covered in tattoos. They both have long hair and huge muscles. They're the types of guys you see on the covers of fitness magazines. And they're confident and tough. In other words, they're everything I'm not.

Mitch lives in California, so we're not exactly close. I don't know him very well at all, I guess, and honestly *no one* really knows me. But Jake, he's absolutely the best. He never gives up trying with me. When the rest of the world decided it had better things to do, Jake stepped in as my protector, advocate, and only friend. So he's a great big brother and way more important to me than I could ever be to him. He basically tackled and shoved my scrawny self into the gym after I moved into my apartment following my altogether undistinguished high school career. He thought it would help me find my confidence; you know, like maybe I dropped it behind the racks of free weights or something.

I'd do almost anything for Jake. I may be stunningly awkward, but I know and appreciate that I won the big-brother lottery. So I started dragging myself out to his gym really early in the mornings, before the crowds come, just to make him happy. As much as I was doing it for him and not for myself, I have to admit, as time has gone on, I've managed to undergo a bit of a post-school transformation as a result of Jake's nagging. I've gradually planked and lifted away some of the gangly awkwardness. I filled out and hardened up—not to Mitch or Jake's levels or anything, but I can definitely see the outside, physical changes for the better that have taken place.

Too bad no amount of cardio or free weights could ever cure the rolling, chaotic mess I've got going on inside my head.

Chapter 2

Lily's Change

MY MIND IS a wild place to be. That rolling chaos—which I'll admit is mostly ping pong balls of self-doubt bouncing around—makes me feel like my head is packed with caffeinated hamsters running on those little wheels. It's full of constant yet ultimately pointless motion…which is why I got totally off-topic here.

I was trying to describe the exact moment the light went out on Lily's face. That morning, I was walking to the gym as usual, although it was a little later than my typical still-dark o'clock. So, it was light enough for me to notice, as I was walking by, that Lily was sitting at a table in a small coffee joint located along my journey. The coffee shop in question, Say Java, has somehow managed to stay afloat despite the fact that Starbucks and its global-domination effort has surely had its fingers wrapped around every competitor's throat for at least the past decade, if not longer. *Of course Lily would support a mom-and-pop shop,* I thought to myself as I caught sight of her and slowed down.

She had an enormous vat of coffee in front of her, and she was talking to a girl she's with a lot. I don't know if they're sisters or friends or coworkers, but I recognize her from the back of her head. Lily's eyes, which I know are a light blue even though I've never been close enough to her to really see for sure—they're so pale it's obvious—were sparkling and flashing with their usual good humor and light. *My sunshine,* I thought to my dopey self as tingling feelings of warmth and everything-is-just-right-ness spread through me simply because I caught a glimpse of her through a shop window.

That's how far gone I am for her. Typically, not much cuts through my worries and fears. Solitude, that calms me. Reading, yeah, that's also a happy escape. And Jake, he reassures and accepts me. But Lily? She *touches* me. When you're as wrapped up inside yourself and are as tightly wound in a ball of issues as I am, you hold onto anything that offers comfort. So yeah, I cling like a koala on a eucalyptus to my crush on this gorgeous woman, who has no idea I'm even alive.

I was about to walk by—I may have problems but I'm not a stalker—when it happened. The smile slid right off her face. Tears started to gather in those bright eyes, making them look even more like shimmering pools than they normally do. Her mouth kind of fell open, as though she was searching for words she couldn't find. And wow do I know *that* sensation. I feel that way anytime I'm forced to interact with anyone for pretty much any reason. So I know it when I spot it.

Whatever her friend had just said hit her like a physical blow. Then she leaned her head forward, which caused the golden brown- and blonde-streaked layers of her long hair to hang down, temporarily blocking her face from my view. I hadn't meant to stop walking, and I knew I needed to get moving before someone called the cops on the pervert staring in the coffee shop window at the beautiful, and suddenly sad, goddess. But I couldn't move. I'd never seen Lily upset before. I thought I'd seen every possible expression in her arsenal, but I'd never seen *this.*

The friend must have been talking still, because I saw Lily shake her head slightly, like she was in denial about whatever was happening or being said. I wanted to know more. What was going on? Why was she upset? I wished in that moment, more than I'd ever wished for anything in my life, that I could comfort her. I would have given absolutely everything to race in, scoop her out of her chair, and wrap my arms around her while she cried. But, really, who was I kidding? No one needs me for that. No one needs me for *anything,* and most certainly not for comfort. I can't even talk to people. So what would be comforting about me freezing up and flailing for words that never came anyway?

It was while I was busy stirring up that inner avalanche of self-recrimination and doubt that it happened: She lifted her head up again, and I could see immediately that it was all just…gone. Her sparkle. Her light. Her sunshine. All of it, completely vanished. She looked utterly devastated. Hardened, even. I felt the urge again to shove through the door and save her somehow. Whisk her away somewhere and find out what was wrong. I could fix whatever the issue was, maybe. Or I could kiss it away, or maybe punch someone for her. Or I could simply hold her hand and talk to her and convince her that everything was going to be okay.

But that was all a joke, wasn't it? How could I possibly fix whatever had devastated that magnificent angel when I couldn't even fix myself? That was the cold, hard truth of the situation, regardless of how much it hurt to have such thoughts carve their way through my mind. I could barely string three words together in any setting; how was I possibly going to be able to find the words to help soothe this beautiful, caring woman?

The answer to that question was both painfully obvious as well as stunningly simple: *I couldn't.*

I let myself take one more lingering look at her precious face, still streaked with pain. Then I forced myself forward again, alone and unseen.

As always.

Chapter 3

The Slump

"I'M IN A SLUMP," I moaned as I absentmindedly stirred the coffee that would hopefully get me through the morning. I always load mine with cream and then tell myself that using sweetener packets offsets the calories. I mean come on…it's practically *good* for me at that point, right? Cream has calcium for my bones and whatnot.

"I love you, sweetie," Claire said, cutting through my fog as she played with her own coffee, which had to be about fifty percent sugar and cream, if not more, so mine was way healthier. "But *slump* implies some sort of downward slide is happening. You have to hit a high spot before you can slump."

"Ouch, kick a sister when she's down," I protested, although Claire had nailed the situation in one try, as usual. She's pretty awesome that way, actually. Claire is that friend who will tell you the truth no matter how painful. I never have to worry that there's toilet paper stuck to my shoe or my skirt is caught in my underwear because she'll tell me. She'll also let me know if I'm being blind to a situation or completely optimistic to the point of stupidity, which is a trap I fall into all the time. Her words can be like arrows piercing the heart of a problem, and sometimes people just don't get her or appreciate the truth bombs. But I adore that quality in her. Everyone needs someone in their life willing to call them out on all their messes and misfires.

"Sorry sweetie, but I speak truth," she said. "You're not in a dating slump. You're in a dating wasteland, flat and barren, that stretches into infinity."

"Oof," I said, laying the coffee stirrer down and looking up at her. "You're in rare form today."

"Yeah, sorry. I really am trying to help here. You know I want more than anything for you to find some dating success."

"I know, but stay positive! Maybe I've already met my person. Maybe the wheels of my epic romance are already in motion." I undramatically capped off the moment with a cautious sip of my coffee, which was still mercilessly hot. The words sounded bold, and I was *trying* to be my usual chipper self. But I'm not going to lie…I really wasn't feeling it.

See, the thing is, Claire's not wrong. I haven't had almost any romantic success in a painfully long time…if ever, come to think of it. In all honesty, I was coming to believe in that moment that I truly irritate men who interest me. Or maybe I annoy everyone I meet; who knows? But at the very least, the men I date are overwhelmed by me. That's got to be it. If it's not, then I *really* don't know what's happening.

Maybe what some people call my friendliness or optimism or bubbly personality might actually be coming off as grating, high-energy blasts of fizzy irritation to the guys I've gone out with. Every time I meet a new guy, just when I start to feel a connection or an attraction, and the moment I'm beginning to let embers of hope spark in my chest that yes, this might actually be a guy who I could really connect with, he'll suddenly throw on the brakes and roll the dating train right back into friendship station.

I mean, it's not like any of these guys have told me

that I drive them crazy. I get all kinds of *other* responses. They pretend that we never even went out and ask about my friends instead. They give long-winded excuses wrapped up as heart-rending backstories—all imaginable variations of "It's not you, it's me." They wax poetic about how hard it is to talk with other women, but how incredibly simple it is to talk with me because I'm their "buddy." They tell me they don't think of me *that way*. Not me, with my natural chattiness and my ability to draw even the quietest of people out of their shells. Nope, not good-old Lily. But really, those qualities are what make me who I am. So, if they don't like the outgoing, bubbly exterior, then I guess they really don't like me after all.

My mom has always said I could get a raincloud to smile. And I always thought that was a good thing, right? Like it's something I'd put at the top of my greatest-hits list. My secret superpower even. But now? Now I'm starting to wonder. I mean, it came from my *mom,* and I know she thinks it's a compliment. But maybe it's not. Maybe the raincloud just wanted to be left alone. Maybe it only smiled so I'd shut up.

I'm not really sure how else to explain why I get automatically slotted into every guy's friendzone. And, no lie, I'm talking *every* guy I've ever gone out with. Seriously. I don't just spend time in the friendzone; no, I live there. I'm the mayor of the friendzone. I'm kissing babies and shaking hands with my friendzone constituents while other women are making passionate, fun-filled connections or finding the loves of their lives.

Claire sighed, cutting through the morose inner dialogue that spun out of control in the awkward silence. Clearly my attempt at romantic bravado fell flat. I looked up at the sound and studied her face, her eyes still turned down with unwarranted fascination at her sugar-bomb drink. Something was off with her, I eventually decided. I'd been so wrapped up in my own angst that I didn't catch the signs. They're subtle, believe me. She's a rock when it comes to showing weakness or emotions. But I know my girl, and it's weird for her to be up this early for one thing. But hey, she's the one who summoned me, claiming she just wanted to see my sunny face. And she's not usually so introspective.

"What's up, Claire-bear?" I asked, nudging her leg under the table with my foot. "I can tell something's bugging you."

"You're not wrong," she replied, looking up now. "I've been trying to find a way to tell you something that you're not gonna want to hear."

"Why not just use your usual frying-pan-to-the-face technique, then?" I asked, trying to tease the worry off her face. "You're not one to hold back."

"Truth," she said, biting her lip now. "It's just…you *really* aren't going to want to hear this. And I don't want to be the one to say it."

"Now you've got me scared," I said. "Tell me what it's about, at least."

"Chad," she finally said, breathing her brother's name out in a frustrated exhale.

My heart dropped.

Chapter 4

The Truth Bomb

"CHAD?" I ECHOED, forgetting the dread as a vision of his handsome face floated through my mind. "Is he sick? Is something wrong?"

"No, no, he's fine. Healthy, anyway," she said. "Still just doing his bachelor-life thing and living to torture me."

"Okaaay...."

Unbelievably awkward silence thudded into the space between us again, but I didn't want her to continue anymore. If she had something bad to tell me about Chad, I really and truly didn't want to know.

The thing is, I've been crushing on him forever. Like *forever* forever. Since the minute his hazel eyes first met mine, which was at her ninth birthday party. He was the very definition of middle-school, skater-dude cool as he brushed the dirty blonde bangs out of his face while indifferently glancing over at me. That was it. I was gone. It was such a dumb, throwaway moment, but it's always lived under a bright spotlight on the stage that holds my memories.

You know that thing that happens when you have a huge crush on someone, and you can just *see* in perfect focus how fantastic you'd be together? That's been me about Chad since that moment. Given time and watered with false hope, those visions in your head grow roots and sprout. Plus, the fact that he's just a super chill guy hasn't stopped my dreams from growing. He helped me move into my apartment, for example, even though I could only pay him in pizza and beer. I've got countless examples like that, which I've carefully collected like they were love letters through the years—little gestures of kindness filed away as markers of what I believed to be his growing feelings for me.

We've even hung out together at various family and social functions. He's really opened up to me about things like college and career goals a few times—something else I took as a sign, forgetting that pretty much everyone opens up to me. No, I filed those chats away in my heart's evidence collection. I've had plenty of time to let this fantasy grow. I mean, come on! It's the classic "my best friend's big brother" trope. No romance fan could possibly have interpreted things any other way. And I'm the very definition of a hopeless romantic.

Claire's always known about my infatuation, although maybe not how much I truly believe we'll end up together. So, whatever she's got to say about him…well, she knows I'm invested.

"What is it?" I finally dared to ask. "He's seeing someone? Is it serious?"

"No," she said. "Definitely not. He had some sort of work function to go to…I don't know, I wasn't listening when he was talking about it the other day. But then suddenly I tuned into him saying he wished he had a date he could bring to whatever it was."

"Okay….," I said again.

"Yeah, well, of course I know how much you like him, so I thought, hey, this might be your chance, right?" She asked it like a question she actually wanted answered, so I nodded in agreement. "You're my girl so

I went for it," she went on, "and I threw your name out there. Like, 'What about Lily?' and he said, 'What *about* Lily?' in a snarky kind of way."

"Oh, ouch," I said, my cheeks flooding with heat. "I mean, that was awesome of you to suggest me. But yeah, you're right—that hurts."

"Lils, I haven't gotten to the bad part," Claire said, sighing again and taking in a deep breath. "I said that maybe he could take you as his date. He said, and I quote, 'I'm not hanging out with a chick who's basically my sister'."

Disappointment swirled through me wildly as Claire shook her head.

"Still not the bad part," she rolled on. She studied me for a minute, then took a deep breath, the words now pouring out of her like a faucet that had been turned on full blast.

"He said you freak him out, Lils, and that you never shut up or stop smiling. This part is a direct quote: *It'd be like dating Tinkerbell riding a unicorn, but with sugar and rainbows somehow involved. There's a reason me and all my friends called her Silly Lily in school, you know.*" Still watching my reaction closely, she lamely added, "End quote."

My mouth flopped open as shock and embarrassment flooded through me. I dropped my head then and closed my eyes behind the curtain of my hair, willing the tears to stop pooling in my eyes. Next came something that ached like shame, and it was all mixing into a tornado tearing through my head, spinning and devouring everything in its path. Like my pride, for example.

"Why?" I finally choked out. "You knew how much that'd hurt. You had to know."

"Girl, *of course* I knew it would hurt," Claire countered, her tone softer than her words. "I've been driving myself crazy trying to decide what to do ever since he opened his big mouth and all that stupid junk fell out. But in the end, I decided you had to know, and know exactly, word-for-word, how brutal it was."

"Why?" I asked again in a weirdly throaty whisper. My head was still down, unable to meet her gaze as his caustic words clanged around in my mind.

"Lils, tell me honestly, would you have wanted to keep grasping onto this torch you carry for my dumb brother forever, never knowing his true feelings?"

I shook my head. Of course I wouldn't.

"That's why I decided I had to tell you. I know how much you like him. I needed you to understand, definitively, that it's never happening. And for you to realize that you wouldn't want it to happen anyway. He's an idiot! I don't want you to hold onto this crush so tightly and so blindly that you miss out on some other great guy who might be out there right this minute, just waiting for someone as wonderful as you are to come along."

"Oh yeah, I'm a real catch," I said, finally looking up to meet her eyes again. The red heat was still coloring my face and the tears were still shining in my eyes. "Zero out of a hundred guys polled would love a chance to date me because I'm a straight-up breath of fresh air. Like a sugared-up pixie, apparently."

"You *are* a breath of fresh air, and that's why I love you so much," Claire told me. "He's *one* guy. One guy with one idiotic opinion. And yes, you've known him a long time, but he doesn't truly know *you.* You can't give too much weight to his ugly words. They don't mean anything."

"They mean something to me, though," I said, reaching for my purse. "Listen, it's getting late. We both need to get moving."

"Lils, I'm sorry," Claire replied, also grabbing her bag as we stood and started clearing off the table.

I waved goodbye to Meadow—one of the crew who normally works there in the mornings—and darted out the door to the sidewalk.

"I'm sorry," Claire repeated from close behind, her words stopping my flight. "You're my best friend. You know I'd never purposely hurt you, at least not without a good reason."

I turned back around and walked woodenly into her outstretched arms.

"I know," I whispered against her shoulder.

Chapter 5

Breakfast with Jake

I CAN'T GET IT off my mind. That look on Lily's face when she lifted her head again is creating a visual echo chamber inside my head. It's been days since it happened, but no matter what I'm doing or thinking, her devastated face is what I'm seeing. For someone as lost inside his own head as me, that's a powerful statement.

"What's going on, bro?" Jake asked, catching me as I walked out of the men's locker room. "You done with your workout?"

"Yeah, heading home," I said. Which was really just stating the obvious, since I'm either home or at the gym. My world is pretty small, something Jake's always on me about.

"You have time for a late breakfast before you go?" he asked, a hopeful look on his face. Jake never stops trying with me.

"You mean a crappy p-protein drink here at the gym?" I asked, pretty convinced I knew the answer.

"Of course!" he roared good-naturedly, thumping me on the back for added effect. "How are we going to keep these manly physiques if we're shoving them full of bacon and pancakes?"

"Riiight," I muttered as I followed him to the drink bar in the corner. He wandered behind the counter and started rummaging around for whatever he puts in those horrifying concoctions. Protein powder? Peanut butter? Dragon tears? I have no idea.

"So, spill it," he said, looking like a mad scientist as he rummaged and gathered the dreadful ingredients.

I raised my eyebrows at him and gave him a universal *What?* look.

He sighed, thumped two tall glasses on the counter between us, and started brewing up the chemistry experiment he was trying so valiantly to pass off as breakfast. I sat on a stool and watched in silence as he worked, a look of dedicated concentration on his face. When he was finally satisfied, he shoved one of the glasses over to me, took a huge gulp from his own, and tried to draw me out again.

"Maxwell, you can hide from the world, but you can't hide from me," he declared with an uncharacteristically steely gaze. "What's wrong?"

My eyes, which were assessing his vaguely green creation, shot back to meet his. "I don't know wh-what you mean," I finally countered.

"Don't play games with me, brother," he insisted, irritation uncharacteristically spiking his words. "You can tell me anything, you know."

"It's nothing," I began cautiously. How did he even know I was upset by the sadness I'd seen on Lily's face? Was I *that* transparent?

"Aha, we're finally getting somewhere," he countered. "You admit there's something to what I'm seeing. *Something* is wrong."

"And wh-what are you seeing?" I asked, not sure I wanted to hear the answer.

He stared at me a long, thoughtful moment before replying.

"Listen, kid, I know things haven't been the easiest for you." He was already leaning heavily into his big-brother mode, something he specializes in—he's forever calling me "kid" even though he's only a few years older than me. "I know you didn't have it easy growing up, and I know Mom and Dad did more damage than good in the big push to 'help' you. But how long are you going to let their mistakes define you, huh? Forever?"

"I-I'm…n-not….," I started, the words getting caught in traffic on the congested highway that runs between my brain and my mouth. As usual. I floundered for a while before admitting defeat with a shake of my head.

A look of—is concerned frustration a normal thing?—crossed Jake's face as he took another drink, all the while studying me like a trigonometry problem.

"Max, I love you enough to say the hard stuff you don't want to hear," he went on finally. "No one else wants to push you or confront you, but that's why you've got me."

"O-okay?" I managed to reply. The end of the word raised up like a question even though I was pretty sure what he was about to hit me with. It was probably going to be some version of the lecture I've heard several times from him and my mom over the years. Well, okay, not my mom anymore, but when she stopped trying with me, Jake picked up the relay baton and ran with it. They either come in hard with *Why don't you go back to speech therapy?* or they offer some version of *Why aren't you getting some counseling?*

I sighed and braced myself for another round.

"I know Dad was too hard on you," Jake started. "He pushed and nagged and belittled you to the point where you just gave up. You were like a boxer who took too many punches and couldn't get off the mat."

Jake paused then to look at me, like he was expecting a reply to what he must have thought was a stunningly brilliant analogy. But come on, it's not like any of what he'd said so far was new territory. We'd been there. We'd talked about it.

How could there possibly be more to say on the subject?

I STUDIED HIM carefully in return before finally offering him a weak shrug. *Yep, I guess we really were going to rehash this, then....* Our whole family knows the basic facts—I developed a minor stutter in elementary school. My parents flipped out in different ways about it. My mom started having me tested, putting me in endless rounds of speech therapy, having me practice via endless conversation with her, and basically turning every other moment of my existence into a speech-correction lab.

My dad, on the other hand, zoomed directly to extreme frustration with almost no stops along the way. He was annoyed with me, with the therapists, with my mom, and with the twist of fate that had led him to become plagued with me. He didn't understand why I couldn't just toss words out like a "normal" kid. He didn't seem to care enough about what I was trying to communicate to put in the time to wait for the words to come. He didn't want a kid who had problems or was different, especially since Jake and Mitch were so impossibly awesome at everything they did that the comparison became especially jarring and painful for him. Jake and Mitch were Best in Show, and I was the runt of the litter.

He got impatient almost from the first day with my seemingly slow progress and by the lack of a cure, and he started taking it out on me. Not physically, but trust me when I say that words can land like punches.

Just spit it out!

The other kids are going to make fun of you if you don't knock it off!

Hazel! What in the world is this boy trying to say?

Why am I paying for all this therapy when this kid still can't string three words together?

His impatience was a powerful force that seemed to sprout tendrils which then wrapped fiercely around my confidence and my progress, eventually choking them like weeds overrunning a garden. The madder he got, the worse my stutter became, until I eventually stopped talking altogether.

Jake knows all of this, of course; it engulfed his childhood, too. I always thought there had to be some parts inside both of my brothers that resented the negativity that my stutter caused in our family. Mitch and I rarely talk, so even though he might be filled with such resentment, he's never directed it at me. I just sort of don't exist much in his world outside the occasional texted meme.

But Jake, he's different. If those bitter feelings are living inside him, he would never reveal them to me. And he would never ignore me, give up on me, or cut me off. It's like he's tied himself inextricably to my emotional well-being. The harsher our dad got, the more I sank inside myself. But as I slid down inside that black hole, Jake reached out and grabbed my hand. He's been holding onto me tightly as I dangled over the abyss since we were kids. It's got to be exhausting; no wonder he works out so much. He needs the strength to keep holding onto me.

"Listen, I know I don't have to rehash everything with you," he said. "I know Mom tried to help you, and

Dad tried to dismantle you, and the whole thing kind of exploded. But you're an adult now, Maxwell. It's time to figure this out for yourself. Maybe try therapy to deal with what has to be a mountain of issues bubbling inside of you, mostly courtesy of Dad. Or focus on trying to make a new friend, talk to a girl, or plan a trip. I don't care what you do, but Max, you have to do *something*. You can't live the rest of your life trapped in that stupid apartment."

"I'm h-here at the gym right n-now," I offered lamely. There wasn't much else about his impassioned speech I could refute because he wasn't wrong. I haven't exactly tried to fix all the broken pieces of myself. I haven't even gotten out a broom to sweep them into a pile. They're just spread around the floor, exactly where they landed when I detonated. Like Legos waiting to be stepped on in the dark.

"Right," he said, a snarky tone in his reply. "And if it wasn't for me dragging you to the gym, you wouldn't be *here* either."

I gave him another shrug. He wasn't wrong.

"Okay, so you started going to the gym for me," Jake said, nodding like he'd just had a good idea. "That's good for a start. Now you have to do something *else*. And if you won't do it for yourself, do it for me. Tell me what's bothering you, and then do something, *anything*, to fix it. To make a change."

He got me there by playing a trump card. I may not be overly motivated to help myself, but I'd do absolutely anything for Jake—and he knows it.

What could I do to wipe that worry off his face, though? What could I even offer him?

I looked down again at the green sludge in the glass in front of me as my thoughts whirled. Jake waited patiently, used to biding his time when it was my turn for a response.

Finally, I lifted my head, took a deep breath, and looked him straight in the eye.

"There's this g-girl I like," I said.

A smile broke across his face.

Chapter 7

Cookie Dough Blues

I THINK Chad's words broke me.

I'll admit I was already in a gloomy headspace about my lack of romantic success way before the Tinkerbell-on-a-unicorn bomb dropped. But I'd been chalking up all my extended-singledom woes to the thought that maybe my outgoing personality was a little too intense for some people. Maybe my sunshine was giving them sunburn instead of warmth. What I hadn't suspected, I guess, was that people just think I'm ridiculous. I want to be thought of as kind and caring and approachable, not someone lacking in substance or depth. And someone not worth getting to know because I'm…silly.

It's been more than a week since Claire said what she said, and I can't stop hearing it. Her words are blasting their way through me constantly, affecting my every thought and action. And the more they bounce around my head, the more they dent my confidence and bruise my self-worth. I wish I could make it all stop, but I can't. I know Claire tried to explain it away as unimportant because Chad doesn't truly know me that well. But that's not how I see it. He knows me well enough. He's certainly known me a very long time; he's known me way longer than anyone I've ever gone out with at least, so I feel like his words carry some weight to them. If he thinks those things about me, he can't possibly be the only one.

Plus, as stupid as this sounds, I'm grieving the death of my crush on Chad, too. I don't think even I fully understood how deep my feelings ran. As illogical as it may be, I must have *really* thought we'd be together one day, because this is hitting me like a true breakup. I just want to cry and listen to sad songs.

As a result, I've been hiding from the world. Well, no...that's an exaggeration because I'm still going to work every day. I'm the receptionist in a dental office, which isn't exactly making a ton of use out of my English degree. But, hey, it pays the bills. And normally I love it. It's kind of perfect for me, really. I'm basically just meeting and chatting with new people all the time. But in the last week or so, I'm there without really being *there*. I find myself talking less to the patients or my coworkers, and I haven't wanted to go out with anyone in the evenings, either. Honestly, I just want to be alone and miserable, rolling around in my morose feelings.

I also stopped writing. I tried a few times to sit at my laptop with every intention of spending time on my beloved hobby, but I'm finding that I just can't come up with the words anymore. Chad's assessment of me is set on full-blast in my head, drowning out all creativity in the process.

It's been a long-cherished dream to write books, specifically romances. Under typical circumstances, writing just pours out of me. That's part of who I am, or at least who I've always thought myself to be. I always seem to have a lot to say, both out loud and on the page. I love talking to people, and that fuels the writing fire. Those conversations spark story ideas, and as a result, I've got scenes and fragments written for countless tales of love. But now that dream is starting to wrap itself up in my self-doubt and embarrassment. I mean, honestly, who wants to read about love from someone too shallow to truly connect with anyone? Maybe true love doesn't even exist for everyone. Maybe some people don't actually get a happily-ever-after. And maybe that'll be *my* story.

I admit I'm getting overly dramatic about the whole thing; I can feel myself doing it. It's like I can stand outside myself, objectively view the tangle of paralyzed embarrassment and identify it for what it is—an overreaction to a bit of criticism. But knowing and being able to back myself out of it are two different things. So I guess I'm still wallowing.

I was spiraling, slumped on the couch eating refrigerated cookie dough right out of the tube with a spoon—exactly what the warnings about eating raw eggs tell you not to do—on a late Saturday afternoon, when my phone chimed its incoming-text alert.

I popped the heaping spoon right into my mouth and held it there like a lollipop to free up my hand as I grabbed the phone and looked at the screen. It was a text from Claire.

Let's go, her cryptic message said.

Huh? I responded, then tossed the phone aside so I could pull the spoon back out of my mouth. Priorities.

The phone chimed again. I sighed, rolled the top of the tube down in a lame attempt to seal it, dragged myself reluctantly off the couch, tossed it in the fridge, then set the spoon in the sink before returning to my non-conversation.

I'm here, she wrote. **Open the door.**

I rolled my eyes as I went to the door—not a long trip in this tiny apartment—and yanked it open to find Claire with her hand on her hip in a stance that screamed impatience intertwined with concern.

"Oh my gosh," she said, walking in. "It's worse than I thought."

"What is?" I asked, glancing down at myself to make sure I didn't have any clumps of dough or chocolate chips stuck to my over-sized t-shirt.

"You!" she said, scanning me up and down. "You look like the poster in a doctor's office where they ask if you've got any of the symptoms of depression."

"I'm fine," I insisted. "Don't be silly...."

I kind of trailed off as soon as I heard that awful word leaving my mouth. *Silly.* Claire's eyes shot up to meet mine. Yeah, thanks universe. She heard it, too.

"You're mad at me," Claire said. "I'm sorry, Lils. I'll say it a million times if I have to, but I am so sorry I told you. I shouldn't have said anything. Your crush on Chad would have died its own inevitable death once you found your real person anyway. I shouldn't have been the one to kill it."

"No, no," I said, shaking my head. "You were right. I'm happy you told me. I wouldn't have wanted to wait forever to figure it out on my own."

"Oh yeah, sure, you *look* super happy, so that tracks," Claire countered, her sarcasm pinging around the room. "And who said anything about forever, anyway? Your man is out there somewhere right this very minute, frustrated he can't find you. And do you want to know *why* he can't find you? Because apparently you intend to hide in your apartment for the rest of your life, with your face shoved in vats of ice cream and self-pity."

"Shows what you know," I said, attempting indignation. "I haven't touched any ice cream in weeks."

"Too busy with cookie dough?" she asked, her face twisted into an expression that was highlighted with one raised eyebrow and could only be interpreted as *Don't lie, because we both know I'm right.*

Okay, so she got me on that point.

"Why are you here?" I asked, trying a different tactic. "I thought you had a second date lined up with...Simon?"

"Sebastian," she corrected. "And I do, but not tonight. Tonight I'm dragging my best friend out of her apartment to try to undo some of the damage I caused."

"I don't feel like going anywhere," I told her. "I think I'm coming down with a cold or something. I just want to lie on my couch and binge all the shows I'm behind on."

"That's literally one of the items on the depression checklist," she said, a fiery look of determination in her eyes. "Get showered. Get dressed. And stop tossing out weak excuses. This is happening."

Chapter 8

The Gaze

LIKE I SAID BEFORE, I know my girl. And I know that look in her eye. There was no way this standoff was going to end with me alone on the couch embracing my cookie dough again. Either she was going to drag me out or she'd end up staying here, chained to my side by the guilt she felt.

I love Claire more than I love my self-pity, I guess, because I gave up and did what she wanted. For the first time since I got home from work on Friday, I took a shower and put on some makeup. When I walked out of the bathroom, I found her pawing through my closet, presumably looking for something a not-depressed person would wear on a Saturday night.

"Where are we going, anyway?" I asked, not caring much but at least a little curious.

"Shopping, apparently," she said, disgust dripping off each word. "You seriously need sexier clothes."

"My current clothes are the exact right amount of sexy."

"Girl, any less sexy and they'd be church-choir robes."

"Ouch. So…jeans then?"

She rolled her eyes as I pulled out a soft pair of boyfriend-cut jeans, a peasant-style shirt, and some cute little ankle boots.

"There!" I said with faked enthusiasm. "Sexy, yet practical."

"Okay," she agreed with a nod and a defeated sigh.

After I got dressed, I grabbed a jacket and then my purse and was soon locking up and heading down the hall, trailing behind her.

"So, what have you been doing with yourself?" she asked while we waited for the elevator. We could easily be in for a long wait since the elevator in my building is notoriously slow. I think people prop it open in the basement when they're getting their laundry or something.

"Nothing, really," I said. This wasn't an exaggeration.

"I hope you've been writing at least," she said encouragingly. No one's more excited about me finally finishing my first book than Claire.

"Nope," I said, popping the *p* sound for emphasis. "I think that phase might be over. I think it was all a pipe dream anyway."

"Girl, *what?*" Claire all but shrieked as the elevator pinged and the doors slowly opened. We climbed inside, and I pressed the button for the lobby. The doors hadn't even closed yet before she continued. "Talk to me. What do you mean it's a pipe dream?"

"Nothing," I said, shrugging weakly. "I don't know, I just...I've got scenes and dialogue fragments and millions of story ideas, but it's just a scattered mess. I don't think it's ever going to come together in one cohesive creation."

"Maybe you need to join a writing group. Or find a writing pal or something," she suggested. "You know, someone to bounce ideas off and hold you accountable for milestones."

"Yeah, maybe," I said noncommittally. "I don't know. It's a ton of work, and I'm just not feeling it.

Plus, I'm no longer sure that romance is my genre anyway."

The elevator opened, and we walked out into the small lobby. It was almost empty, although I couldn't help noticing two guys over by the mailboxes. I'm not super observant, but the lobby is really small for as many tenants as we have.

"What do you mean it's not your genre?" she asked. "You've been into it for as long as I've known you. You've always wanted to do this. What's changed?"

I let the question fall between us as I studied her face. I didn't want to heap any more guilt on her shoulders, but I also didn't want to lie.

"Well?" she prompted. "Why would romance suddenly not be your genre anymore?"

"You can't write romance if you don't believe love can happen for everyone," I finally replied, my words sort of choking me up at the end.

"Oh, get out of here with that," she shot back, looking angry now. She dug around her purse for a minute before handing me a tissue. "You need a partner. A writing buddy. That's all. I'm certain that would help you get out of this funk."

"I couldn't help but overhear," one of the guys by the mailbox suddenly interjected, turning toward us now. I dabbed my eyes with the tissue as Claire and I both looked at him. His long hair was pulled up into a man bun, and tattoo sleeves covered what I could see of his arms. The muscles were all but bulging out of his t-shirt, which looked like it was hanging on for dear life. *His whole vibe screams spicy romance book cover, come to think of it.* "You're looking for a writing buddy?" he asked.

"She is!" Claire chirped before I could even create

meaning from the words he'd uttered. He was so shockingly gorgeous that it was hard to focus, honestly. "Are you a writer?"

"No, I'm not a writer, but my, uh, friend is," he said, a relaxed, sexy smile on his face. "It's a crazy coincidence, but he's been looking for someone to write with, too."

"Oh, really? Um…I don't know…," I started, as I looked from his magnificent face to Claire's, where I saw nothing but triumph in her expression. My thoughts got tangled up in a bit of a panic then, so I tried to glance back toward Tattoo Guy instead.

This time, however, my eyes landed on the face of the other guy. He actually seemed a little familiar, I thought as I did an embarrassingly cartoon-like double-take on him. He was both familiar and…just…*wow*. He was every bit as hot and almost as ripped as the first guy, but without the cool-dude swagger. Definitely he wore his hotness in a quieter, more understated way. No man-buns or tattoos that I could see. No, his most striking features were his soulful, deep-brown eyes, which utterly transfixed me. The threads of the conversation dropped from my mind as I let my gaze linger in his a few more moments, unable to look away. *If this was a movie,* I thought, *this scene would be shot in slow motion.* My eyes wandered for a second down to his mouth before rolling up to his eyes again. I could feel my heartbeat accelerating, and my breaths suddenly felt shallow as the moment stretched out.

"Do you have his contact information?" Claire asked Tattoo Guy, startling me with a nudge and, like a needle scratching across a record, finally breaking my near-hypnotic trance. The entire exchange, from our steps off the elevator to when she elbowed me, probably only lasted thirty or forty seconds, tops. Somehow, though, the moments I'd spent transfixed by Soulful Guy felt like they had stretched out lazily into infinity.

"Wh-what?" I asked, looking over at her again. I'd gotten so lost in his eyes that I'd completely forgotten what we were talking about. Honestly, I'd even forgotten where I *was* for a moment. There was something so mesmerizing and calming in his presence, where I'd gone from dabbing tears away to forgetting I had any problems in the first place. Whatever Soulful Guy was transmitting to me in his heated gaze, I knew one thing for sure: I wanted more of it.

"Here, I'll give you his number," Tattoo Guy was saying. I still couldn't move, so she grabbed my phone out of my hand and typed in the number. "His name is…Cruz."

"Okay great. C-r-u…z?" Claire asked, saving the contact for me as he nodded. "Thank you so much! You have no idea how perfect this is. Warn Cruz he'll be getting a text from Lily soon."

"I will," he said, still smiling his sexy smolder at us as Claire tugged me to follow her out the door. I thought about thanking him, too. But I got snared again in the gaze of the other guy who, I realized later, had never said a word.

Chapter 9

The Plan

"WHAT WAS *THAT?!*" I demanded, my emotions blasting the words right out of me with none of my usual hesitations.

"You're welcome, little brother," Jake said through a self-satisfied chuckle.

"Are you m-messing with me?" I asked.

Before we ran into Lily, Jake had managed to get the whole story out of me about my crush on her—everything down to the moment I saw her get devastated by…well, whatever had happened. Then suddenly she was there, emerging from the elevator as though I'd manifested her from thin air. I elbowed Jake, and I tilted my head toward her. He saw her and…I swear I don't know what happened next. Jake started talking to Lily's friend, and then my eyes locked with Lily's and…I don't know. Absolutely everything else in reality fell away.

"My baby brother's got game!" Jake crowed as he started toward the elevator. "And excellent taste in women, I might add. Your girl is hot!"

"She's n-not m-m-m…," I started before giving up. Jake—and what happened moments before with Lily, if I'm being honest—had me completely flustered.

"Listen," he finally said when it became clear I wouldn't try to finish my thought, "you're over here saying she's not yours. But I was there, Maxwell. I saw the whole thing. Her eyes landed on you, and she was *gone.* She may not be your girl yet, but she sure *could* be."

"You kn-know that's not true," I said, following him into the elevator after it finally arrived. "I could n-never talk to her."

"Sure you can." He put one arm around me and gave me a side-hug. "I just set the ball rolling for you."

"N-no you didn't. What, you t-told her I'm a writer? I'm supposed to write w-with her? I'm not a writer, Jake!"

"Aww, really?" he replied in one of those patronizing tones that only a sibling would ever use. Then the elevator stopped to let us out on my floor. "You can't just get to know her over text or email? Well, I guess you won't mind if I ask her out instead then, huh?"

A tsunami of anger surged inside me, even as Jake cut it off with another chuckle.

"I'm *joking,* Max, chill out," Jake said as I unlocked the door and went in. "Seriously bro, just messing with you. But honestly, I don't think I'd get anywhere with her anyway. I was standing right there, but her big, blue anime eyes could only see you. I'm telling you, she was *into* you. You don't even need to use my writer lie. Just introduce yourself. Your chemistry with her was poppin'. Trust me, bro, you got this."

"N-no," I said, shaking my head. "I c-can't."

Jake sighed dramatically as he flopped down on my couch. "Maxwell, if you've never listened to a thing I've had to say before, at least listen to me now."

"O-okay," I said, sitting across from him in the recliner.

"You're stuck," he began, his joking tone now long gone. "You know these words are heading to you wrapped up in all kinds of big-brother love and concern. But Max, you're stuck inside your head and your own self-doubt. You're stuck inside this apartment. You're stuck in the past, still listening to all the garbage Dad had to say. You're *stuck,* and until you admitted to me that you've got your eyes on this girl, I didn't see how we were going to be able to shove you out of your comfort zone. But now I see it very clearly."

I raised my eyes in a look that surely conveyed extreme doubt…and okay, maybe it was mixed with a touch of hope.

"Your feelings for Lily," he went on, pausing with drama dripping off each word, "are the dynamite that we're going to use to blast you out of this prison."

*   *   *

A moment of stunned silence dropped heavily after his declaration as I worked to process his meaning.

Blast me out of prison?!

"M-maybe *you* should b-be the writer," I finally replied, studying the earnest zeal I could read on his face. Jake *really* believed in that moment he was onto something.

"Bro, stop with the cynicism and just listen to me here. You're stuck. I think that when she saw you, both of you knew in an instant that you have crazy chemistry. *I* think you could walk right up to her and introduce yourself, and then the two of you could walk off into the sunset together and go make cute babies with big eyes. But clearly *you* don't think that. So let's fix this problem. You need to start believing it could happen."

"How?" I asked almost in a whisper. He was so right. I wanted those things. That silly little wisp of a future he'd painted was so tantalizing I could almost feel her hand in mine. But he was also right that I'd never be able to just walk up to her and start talking. *Never.*

"Here's what you're going to do: Text her back when she reaches out to you," he said. "That part's easy. Strike up a friendship. Get to know her. Read up about writing romance books or whatever she's into so you can give her some good advice. But mostly just get to know her. Let her get to know the real you."

"O-okay. But she's g-going to think I'm s-some guy n-named C-Cruz. Why'd you g-give her our last name?"

"I don't know," Jake shrugged. "I didn't want to get too far from the truth, but I was hoping you'd introduce yourself as Max to her once you guys inevitably run into each other again. She'll recognize you now, you know. She's going to want to talk to you after the way you two just made passionate eye-love together."

Pure panic shot through me at the thought of running into her and being unable to chat and flirt like a normal guy. What would she think? How would she react? That chemistry Jake was talking about would never be strong enough to make her get past my awkwardness. I would never want to see disgust in her eyes, but surely that emotion or something similar to it—maybe even pity—is what she'd feel. I shuddered at the thought.

"Chill, you're mentally spinning out," Jake said, accurately reading the emotions on my face. "Use this time wisely. Get to know her in texts. Let her get to know you in return. But also do more than that. Go back to counseling. Or speech therapy. Or both, maybe.

Push yourself. Practice talking to strangers. Walk into a store and place an order or ask a question. Stop doing every transaction online. You have to get past the idea that the only person you can talk to is me. Like I said, if you're going to get out of your prison, it's gonna take more than a little bit of work. It's gonna take an explosion."

I sat back and closed my eyes, letting his words soak into my brain. *Get to know her by texting her—where I'm not forced to speak to her. And in the meantime, work on myself.* Could I do it? Was it possible?

As these questions and many others swirled around my mind, a sudden realization occurred to me. Before, when we were downstairs, Lily had *seen* me. There were four of us in that lobby, but it was *my* eyes she'd locked onto. For the first time in…forever?...I hadn't been ignored. She didn't pass right by without acknowledging me. I hadn't gone unnoticed. Standing next to Jake and all his tattoos and muscles and hair, she'd singled *me* out.

I opened my eyes again and leaned forward.

"I'll do it," I announced.

"GIRL, WHAT WAS *THAT?!*" Claire shrieked the moment the door closed, breaking the spell that was cast when I first glanced at Soulful Guy.

I couldn't find the words to respond because I didn't know what had just happened myself. It sort of felt like all my cells and synapses had been thrown into a blender along with a bolt of lightning. Is static electricity a human emotion? If it wasn't before, I guess Soulful Guy and I just invented a thing, because that's the only way I can think of to describe the tingly awareness I still felt surging and crackling inside me, like a kid with a sparkler lighting up the night. "Ooh, that was crazy!" Claire went on, oblivious to my internal sparkler-ing. "And hot! It was *crazy* hot!"

"I don't know what you're talking about," I replied, not quite ready to dissect it with her. It felt too…private? And almost too *important,* somehow.

Claire stopped suddenly, causing me to walk on a few steps before realizing we weren't together anymore. I spun back to find her gaping at me, incredulity shining in her eyes.

"What?" I finally asked as she continued her over-the-top stare. "Why don't *you* tell *me* what that was? You want me to reach out to some strange guy about my writing? Seriously?"

"Yes, I do," Claire said. "You're going to stop moping around, you're going to text Cruz and start writing again, and you're going to find that hot guy in there and get his name and number!"

"Nah, he's not my type," I said, deliberately being obtuse. "You know I have a thing about man-buns."

"Oh, nice try, but don't play games with me," Claire snapped. "You know I'm not talking about the sexy rock star tattoo guy."

"Claire, I love you, and I love that you're trying to pull me out of my funk," I said as we started walking toward the parking lot again. "And I don't blame you one bit for telling me about them, but I'm still reeling from Chad's words. I don't want to text random guys I don't know, I don't want to write, and I don't want to fan the flames of a new crush on someone only to find out *he* thinks I'm annoying, too. Or only to have him crown me Queen of the Friendzone. I'm just done."

"Chad, Shmad," she said with a wave of her hand, unlocking her car with the remote and climbing inside. I sighed, tugging open the creaky passenger door and joining her. She drove a beat-up Corolla that had only featured one hubcap for years. She was constantly finding "Sell Us Your Junk Car!" flyers on it. "Forget about Chad. Focus on sexy quiet guy because I *know* you were attracted to him. I got a suntan from the heat you two were generating!"

"Fine, yeah, we had a moment there," I conceded, hoping it would be enough to appease her. "If I see him around the building again, I'll definitely say hi."

"Say hi. Right. Because that attraction you two had was so very low-key. Stop lying to me about how awesome and earth-shaking it was. You and your zinging hormones need to scour that building in search of him. Hire a private investigator! Or, wait—duh—you could just ask Cruz about him!" She threw the car into drive and made a right out of the parking lot—in the direction of one of the malls, I assumed. We live in Hackensack, New Jersey, which is close to a ridiculous number of shopping malls. "If he knows man-bun guy, then he surely knows your silent guy. You could easily find out his name and where he lives!"

"I can't think of a single way that would possibly come up in casual text conversations with a stranger," I said, rolling my eyes. "It's not necessary, anyway. The building isn't *that* big. Surely I'll just see him in the laundry room or something. And if you were so worried about my zinging hormones, why'd you drag me out of there so fast?"

"Ugh, fine, you're right, I'm an idiot. I was just so happy to see you *not* moping that it kind of short-circuited my brain. But back to my original point: You *are* going to text Cruz, right? Let's at least get that ball rolling."

"I'll think about it," I said noncommittally.

"No, girl, you'll talk yourself out of it," she argued. "Just do it now, please."

"What? No, I don't even know what I'd say. Plus, he probably hasn't even gotten the heads up about it from his friend yet. This literally happened about two minutes ago, remember?"

"You're making it too complicated," she shot back. "Aren't you the same person who can talk to almost anyone, in any setting? Surely you can reach out to this one random guy and not come off like a stalker. Just be breezy. You know, like, 'Hey, you wanna write wit' me, or what?!'."

I couldn't stop the embarrassing half-laugh, half-snort that erupted from me in response to this ridiculous suggestion, and I smiled at her as gratitude for my goofy and wonderful friend wrapped itself tightly around me.

"Okay, okay, I'll text him now," I conceded, pulling out my phone and starting to type as I read the words aloud. *"Hi, my name is Lily. Your frien….* Oh, wait, why didn't you get Tattoo Guy's name? I can't say *Your friend Tattoo Guy gave me your name."*

"Sorry, I didn't think of it. Your cute little not-moping moment fried my brain, remember? But I think it's okay if you're vague. *He* knows who his friend is, right?"

"Okay, yeah, I guess," I said, looking back at the words I had so far. *"Your friend gave me your name. He said you might be interested in finding a writing partner.* Good?"

"That works," Claire replied, flipping on the blinker for the exit that would take us to the largest nearby mall, which everyone refers to as "The Plaza." "Hit send before you talk yourself out of it."

"But is there enough context? Shouldn't I ask him what kind of writing he does or something? Maybe ask why he wants a writing partner or how he would envision this working?"

"Are you interviewing him for a job, or are you simply making initial contact?"

"The latter, of course," I said, still reading and reviewing the words on the screen. "Ugh, this is so awkward. I haven't even had a minute to think about whether or not I even *want* a writing buddy. You're pushing me too hard and too fast."

"You do want one," Claire insisted, a severe slow-down in traffic allowing her to turn and meet my eyes. "Hit send, Lils. I love you like a sister and know you better than almost anyone, right? I'm telling you right now, as your best friend, that I can feel deep down inside my soul that I'm right here. You absolutely *have* to send it."

I watched her as the words marched confidently from her mouth and made their way to my doubting ears, her tone matching the serious glare she shot me before switching her attention back to her driving. I studied her profile a moment, took a deep breath, and turned back to read the words again. Maybe she was right. Maybe I needed to mix things up and try something different. The status quo sure wasn't getting me anywhere, and that was true long before the Chad thing even happened.

I read my message one last time.

Then I sent it.

Chapter 11

The Response

"*YES!* THAT'S AWESOME!" Jake whooped, hope and pride mingling together and beaming from his face. All that excitement, just because I said I'd attempt to start taking baby steps toward helping myself. I was momentarily blown away by how far I must have fallen if the mere *idea* of me doing something like ordering fast food in person gave my brother so much joy. Then I swatted that thought aside quickly, before it could undermine my decision to try and therefore derail his happiness.

"You're a g-great b-brother," I said, feeling unusually sappy. Actually, I felt off-kilter in general. The interaction with Lily had recalibrated my system.

"You are too, Maxwell," he said, nodding. "The best!"

"W-wait 'til I tell your t-twin that," I said, even as I heard my phone ping with an incoming text. I don't have friends, and the one person I typically hear from was currently beaming at me from my couch. So the sound of an incoming text was a pathetically unusual event.

I grabbed my phone, only to see Lily's name jump out at me.

"It's L-Lily," I said, slowly looking up at Jake with astonishment and terror.

"And just like that, he's got her number," Jake replied, standing up now. "I think my work here is done! Write back to her as Cruz, but don't drag that out forever. Get to work on yourself *today*. Try to get to the place mentally where you can tell her the truth as quickly as possible so this whole ruse doesn't make her mad and ruin your chances with her. You need to do absolutely everything you can to grab your happiness from the jaws of our rotten childhoods. It's time, Maxwell. You are your *own* man, not whoever or whatever Dad thought you should or shouldn't be. Promise me you're going to take this opportunity and run with it. Go on—promise."

As though the mere mention of our dad brought with it the ghosts of the past, I could suddenly hear the old man's voice in my head, still ringing with disappointment and annoyance—

What's wrong with this kid?

Why can't you be normal, like your brothers?

Could someone just tell me what he's trying to say?

I can't stand to listen to him splutter another second.

Save it, M-M-M-Max. I don't have the time or the patience to wait forever for whatever it is you're trying to say to me right now. It's probably not that important anyway.

I exhaled slowly as I worked to drown out his voice with my new inner resolve. Then I looked back down at the text, eyeing Lily's name as though it was a talisman against the past. I was suddenly aware that I was nodding in agreement with Jake's words, before I even realized that's what I was doing.

"I p-promise," I said, looking up again.

"You got this," he reminded me, opening the door to leave, "now respond to her text."

"I w-will," I said solemnly as he closed the door and was gone.

I reached over and twisted the lock, then returned

to the recliner, staring at Lily's text the entire time. *I have her number!* I shouted in my overexcited mind. Glee and wonderment mixed with terror and dread. Standing between me and utter happiness was the knowledge that Lily didn't know that *I* had her number. She thought she was reaching out to Cruz, the fun writing buddy who specialized in finding the right words, rather than Max, the anxiety tornado who couldn't talk. But since that same anxiety tornado was the person currently holding the phone and needing to respond to her, I had to pull myself together fast.

She didn't know me, and she didn't know Cruz either. So, for once, I had a clean slate. The rare opportunity to reset and be who I wanted to be rather than who I already was. I felt like a kid who moved to a new school and now had the chance to reinvent himself. But reinvent myself *how,* exactly? Who did I want to be? Underneath the worries and the constant hunt for words that wouldn't come, *who was I...?*

Well...I guess what I wanted was to be an anchor, the way Jake had always been for me. Someone strong who people—okay, who was I kidding here, not people: *Lily*—could trust and rely on. I wanted to be able to interact freely with absolutely anyone, but especially with Lily. I wanted to be able to articulate the funny things that popped into my head and then listen to her laugh in response. I wanted us to have inside jokes so we could catch each other's eyes across a room and just *know* what the other was thinking. I wanted her to tell me absolutely anything, and for me to be able to do the same with her.

I wanted to be part of an *us*.

All of my wishes and wants revolved around open and easy communication, and the irony of that wasn't lost on me. Communication—or, more specifically, a *lack* of communication—was what started me on my downward spiral all those years ago. I guess it made sense that I wanted a world where I could talk easily and freely and finally be heard.

I looked again at the text she sent me:

Hi, I'm Lily. Your friend gave me your name and number. He said you might be interested in finding a writing partner?

My thumbs hovered over the keys as uncertainty paralyzed me. This was my clean slate, my first day at a new school. No expectations. No preconceived notions. No judgment or exasperation. Just…me. And Lily.

My thumbs started to tap out a reply as if they had a mind of their own.

Hi, yeah. Jake told me about you. He's right. I'm very interested.

Before I could ponder it further, I hit send.

Chapter 12

Writing Buddies

CLAIRE WAS DRAGGING me from store to store in the mall when the first text from Cruz arrived.

"He wrote back!" I said as Claire pawed through a rack of dresses I'd never wear or, for that matter, afford. "Um, yeah—forget those. Too...everything."

"What'd he say?" she asked, rolling her eyes but actually listening and moving on to the next rack.

"Just that yeah, he's interested," I said. "Oh, and the tattoo guy's name is Jake."

"That fits him," she observed, holding a cropped t-shirt up to me and eyeing it critically. "He's so hot. Why weren't your baby blues glued on him instead of that quiet guy?"

"I don't know, honestly," I said. "I mean, of course I noticed the tatt...Jake. I mean, c'mon. He's an infinity on a scale from one to ten."

"You speak truth," Claire replied, holding up another shirt and eyeing me again. "Okay, so then why the passionate eye-lock on the other guy?"

"I really don't know. I swear to you that lightning hit my brain the second I saw him. Our gazes met, and in an instant I wasn't feeling so bad anymore. I was...electrified and soothed all at the same time, which I know doesn't sound like something that's even possible. He's just...sizzling chemistry in human form, I guess, and I was powerless to fight it."

"Nah," she said, shaking her head now. "Nope. He

isn't that at all. I mean, yeah, he's hot, too, but I swear I didn't even notice he was in the room at first. It's not him. It's the two of you *together.* You've got mad chemistry with him, Lils."

"Maybe," I said with a shrug. "I know I've never felt anything like it before, that's for sure."

"Remember I told you that your man was out there somewhere trying to find you, if only you'd leave your apartment?"

"Yeah...." I was pretty sure I knew where she was heading with this.

"Turns out he was waiting for you down in the lobby!" she replied, the triumph clear in her tone and expression. "I was right!"

"I don't know what to do with that information," I said with a laugh, shaking my head and giving her a thumbs-down at the skirt she was currently holding.

"Try to find your chemistry guy. You have to! And write back to Cruz. I need my Lily to be a happy, writing Lily. Got me?"

Now it was my turn to roll my eyes.

"Yeah, I got you."

*   *   *

When we left the mall, I was holding a few shopping bags. She'd talked me into a skirt, a couple of shirts, and a dress that, I had to admit, made me look and feel a whole lot sexier than the "sugared-up pixie" image Chad-via-Claire had tried to plant firmly within my self-confidence. I felt a tiny bit of smug victory as Claire and I climbed back into her junker.

"I feel better," I said, pulling the groaning door closed. "Thanks Claire-bear."

"It was the least I could do. So where to? Dancing in the city?"

By *in the city* she meant Manhattan. But I definitely wasn't up for club-hopping, or even dive-bar sulking.

"If I swear on a stack of Bibles that I will absolutely go home and text Cruz while finding random excuses to wander around my building looking for Hot Chemistry Guy, will you let me call it a night?"

I must have gotten lucky and actually said the magic combination of words, because, with very little pushback from Claire, I soon found myself alone on my couch, phone in hand, pondering Cruz's text. I still wasn't sure what to say. After all, Claire had shoved me into the whole "writing buddy" thing before I could even think about it.

As I sat there mulling it over, though, I could see that she was onto something. My writing had been fairly directionless long before I got blindsided by Chad's true opinion of me. I had dreams of putting a book together, I had some natural talent, and I had a true love of writing. But all that those elements had netted me so far when stirred together with some effort was an enormous collection of snippets and vague story ideas. Nothing was fully fleshed out. I was like a story-starter generator rather than an actual writer.

I took a deep breath and released it slowly as I started to type out a reply.

I confess my friend Claire is the one who came up with this idea, so I don't know exactly how this might work. Do you? All I know is I have a ton of story ideas, no organization for any of them, and, at the moment, a severe mental block.

It accurately summed up the situation, even if I had essentially put figuring it all out back on his shoulders. I hit send.

Then I sat lost in thought for a while. Eventually my phone lit up with a new text.

I've got a ton of disorganized ideas and mental blocks of my own, so we may be onto something here.

His response made me smile. Hopefully he was right, and hopefully the "something" would be beneficial for both of us. Perhaps even great.

Okay then, let's try this, I replied.

Chapter 13

Sherpas

LIKE I REMINDED JAKE, I'm not a writer. But I do understand needing to get yourself organized so you can reach an objective.

I've been doing freelance web design for a couple years now. Web design is all about the stressful combination of painstaking upfront planning and thoroughly understanding the customers' goals for each site. Without that kind of slow and methodical strategy, no one in my business gets very far. Clients won't be happy with the final results, and their customers will be frustrated, too. All of that can lead to bad online reviews, which is something a freelancer like me can't afford to accumulate.

Lily said she had lots of disorganized ideas, and it was very clear to me in that moment that what she needed was a mapped-out strategy like the ones I create for my clients. I may not be successful in almost any other part of my life, but *that* is something I know how to do.

I felt a little giddy, realizing that Jake's machinations actually got me to a place where I could help her. Her words *let's try this* stared back at me from my phone as I thought more about how to respond. I'd agonized over my previous text, laboriously hunting for the right words just like when I'm speaking. The thing is, I didn't want to lie to her any more than I needed to. It was bad enough she didn't know that Cruz was actually Max

Cruz, her ghost of a next-door neighbor who she had never noticed in the entire time she lived there. Well, until she saw me in the lobby, that is—something I really hadn't been able to make sense of yet. All I knew for sure was that I didn't want to start pretending to be a writer. The only things I ever wrote, aside from emails, were headings and captions and buttons and drop-down menus—all the typical text for websites. But I didn't want her to find out I'm not a writer and then stop wanting to chat with me, either.

So I needed a plan, with the end goal to keep talking with Lily, of course. I didn't want to lie about being a writer, but I had to throw something out there that she could help me with so the relationship seemed like a true partnership. What I really needed was help with my social skills, but how honest I could be about that without freaking her out was another matter. I lined up these facts and worries and shuffled them through my mind like a deck of cards before finally deciding on a way to proceed—and hopefully to save the situation.

Here's the thing—Jake wasn't quite on target when he called me a writer. Actually, I'm a web designer. But I think a lot of the skills and organizational strategies that someone needs as a web designer are likely pretty similar to those a writer needs, too.

I was terrified my words would cause her to tell me that this wasn't going to 1work. But my desire to be honest with her was stronger than my fear, apparently, because I hit send without much hesitation. Then my nerves instantly ratcheted up to crazy levels, of course. I started pacing back and forth as I waited for her response, my every cell tuned in anticipation toward the text app. Thankfully, she responded to me much more quickly than I had responded to her, saving me from full-blown cardiac arrest—

Oh yeah, that makes sense, I guess, about how the processes might be similar. But this doesn't seem very fair. How would I be helping you?

Great, now I had to figure out how honest I needed to be about *that* question. Should I tell her that what I was trying to organize and improve was my entire life? That while she was working to form sentences and turn them into paragraphs, then chapters, and then eventually into finished books, I was trying to form a life wherein I was a fully functioning adult who could interact with humanity in a way that didn't involve my laptop? That my goal for the future was to grow so much as a person that I could maybe one day be the kind of man she could see herself dating or even—dare I say it—loving?

Okay, yeah, that would be *too* honest.

I struggled with how much of that truth bomb to drop on her, and eventually came around to a toned-down reply—

I think the reason Jake thought you'd be helpful for me is because I'm currently working on a project, something I've been stuck on for a really long time. He wants to see me get out of that rut.

There, I decided. Honest yet vague, and entirely devoid of any specifics about my struggles. Again, I hit send without mulling it over too long, anxious to hear her response. Which was—

I mean...I guess? I'm pretty much in a rut too, though. I wasn't kidding about that. Not sure I'm the sherpa you're looking for to help you climb out of any ruts, but hey it doesn't hurt to try.

I chuckled at the sherpa image she'd created. I'd seen her laughing a lot in the past, so it definitely tracked to find out she was funny. This bit of humor from her had me responding much more quickly than before—

We can be each other's sherpas. Wait, is that a thing? Do sherpas have sherpas?

Her response was quick too—

Hmm, probably not. But I think it's okay to invent it. It can be OUR thing.

And just like that, Lily and I had *OUR thing*. Wow...my dream of having inside jokes with her was already on its way to becoming a reality, thanks to Jake.

I mentally thanked him before typing out my next reply—

Okay, so tell me more about your rut....

Chapter 14

Getting Wild

Lily: Well...there's a whole lot of backstory to my life here in the rut.

Me: I'm not trying to pry, I swear!

Lily: I know. But hey, sherpas need context. Um...I'll skip that backstory stuff and just say that I've always wanted to write romance books. But certain events have me wondering if...you know what, forget that part, too. Basically, I've got a lifelong dream, a collection of writing that isn't a coherent story, and a boatload of self-doubt.

Me: Self-doubt? You have definitely come to the right place. Not to brag, but I invented self-doubt.

Lily: Wow I'm impressed.

Me: Trust me, don't be. But it's easier to see solutions when you're not part of something. So it feels obvious, to me anyway, that you should try to pick out a single story idea and start mapping out a plan for it.

Lily: Like an outline?

Me: Yeah.

Lily: I hear what you're saying, but I've always been more of a pantser.

Me: Uh....

Lily: That's writer lingo for someone who doesn't plot out a story. They just dive in and write by the seat of their pants. Get it?

Me: Hmm. I am so not a pantser, in anything I do or say.

Lily: Lol.

Me: I get that you prefer that style, but are you sure you don't want to get wild and see how the other half lives?

Lily: Just to make sure I'm clear on this—when you say "wild," you mean to outline everything I write first and do nothing spontaneously?

Me: Yes, that kind of wild.

Lily: More lol.

Me: This will probably have a bunch of text tone I don't intend, but it seems like your pantser lifestyle hasn't gotten you where you want to be, right?

Lily: Ouch.

Me: Sorry!

Lily: No, #truth. Okay, I guess that's where we'll start my side of the journey then, huh?

Me: Abandoning your pantser lifestyle?

Lily: Yeah, I guess so. I'll work on choosing a story idea to outline.

Me: Victory!

Lily: Now, Mr. Hasalltheanswers, what are we going to do about you and YOUR rut?

For once in my life, the words during this entire exchange had been flowing quickly and easily from my brain. I'd never had the opportunity to have a conversation like this in texts before, what with not having any friends and all, and I was rapidly starting to love it. It seemed to be loosening me up and helping me get out of my own head for a change. Plus, it kind of felt like we clicked in some way, and that maybe it wasn't merely the texting that was loosening me up—it was Lily herself. I paused to say a silent, pleading prayer that all of this wasn't just my imagination.

Imagination or not, however, Lily's last question had all my newfound ease screeching to a halt. What could I possibly say about my own rut that wouldn't send her racing away while simultaneously blocking my number? My issues were not in the same realm as hers. She was in a rut, whereas I was in one of those ocean trenches that are too deep to be fully explored. Still…I wanted to continue staying as closely aligned with the truth as possible. After all, none of this would provide a chance to have a real relationship with her if she wasn't getting to know the real me. And if she was, then, well…I had to reveal, for better or for worse, all of my issues. But, of course, I couldn't dump all that at her feet on our very first day of contact.

Suddenly I realized she'd texted again while I was agonizing—

Lily: You still there?

Me: Yeah, sorry. Got distracted.

Lily: If you need to go, we could talk again another time.

I decided to grab this opportunity to give myself more time to think about what part of my life I should offer up as the rut she could help me escape.

Me: Sounds good. When works for you?

Lily: Most evenings, sadly.

Me: Yeah, well, double sad I guess, because that works for me, too.

Lily: Okay great. Thanks, Cruz!

I gave her last comment a thumbs up, then sat there and reread the entire thread a couple times. Okay, yeah, more like a couple hundred times. I still couldn't believe I was chatting with her, and I *really* couldn't believe I was finding it so easy. I'd never chatted with anyone like this even once in my life. She must have some kind of magic inside her, I decided, because even texting her was a soothing balm on my otherwise anxious mind. Another thought—a really good one—sparked through my brain just then like a shooting star. *If merely texting her feels this great, what would actually being with her feel like?*

I quickly snapped that idea shut before it could grow roots or begin hatching little hope babies inside of me. I needed to slow down and take this one step at a time. Yeah, we'd had one text chat. One *amazing* text chat. But that was all. I couldn't flip out and make it more than it was. At a bare minimum, I needed to remember that it certainly meant more to me than it did to her.

I tossed my phone aside and scrubbed my hands over my face with a sigh. I'd told her she needed to outline a story, as though I had the answers to anything.

I guess I needed to take my own advice and plan out what exactly to tell her.

Chapter 15

New Crush

WOW, OKAY, Cruz was fun to talk with. So fun, in fact, that I'd gotten through the entire evening without doing a shame-crawl back to my cookie dough or even thinking about my sugar-pixie status. *Take that, Chaaad,* I thought smugly as I stretched, stiff from lying in one position for so long while I was volleying texts back-and-forth with Cruz.

Cruz.... Yeah, I'd really enjoyed chatting with him, plus he'd given me some pretty solid advice. I mean, it wasn't exactly earth-shattering, what he'd proposed. But sometimes you're so far up in your own head that you need even the most obvious things pointed out to you. Yes, I'd always considered myself a pantser. But no, it didn't seem to be getting me anywhere close to achieving my dreams of writing entire books. I mean, come on, I hadn't even created two chapters in a row yet. There's a perfectly legitimate reason for that, though—what typically happens is that I meet someone new, and suddenly our simple interaction sends my mind spiraling wildly, pulling on story threads from the fabric of their lives. I say hello at the grocery store to a frazzled woman with a crying baby? Boom! A single-mom romance starts writing itself in my mind. I meet a hot-looking older guy at the gas station, and bam! An age-gap tale is unwinding at dizzying speeds in my brain.

When these story kernels start popping, I go home

and immediately begin committing that day's burst of inspiration into written form. But before each particular idea can move from a simple snippet into an actual plot, I've encountered another fascinating person who ignites yet another tale-starter for me. That's how I ended up with such an expansive assortment of story fragments in the first place. Each one is beautiful to me, but none of them have succeeded in getting me anywhere close to a fully realized manuscript. Now that I've created this vast collection of seedlings, how do I even begin to choose one to outline and explore further? What criteria would I even use to select one?

Well…for sure it would need to be an idea strong enough to be worthy of an entire plot and, of course, power-packed with plenty of conflict and chemistry.

Chemistry. The second that word floated through my thoughts, a vision of the silent and soulful-looking guy from the lobby sprang into my head. Now *that* was a great example of powerful chemistry! We hadn't just sizzled; we exploded. But why hadn't he said anything to me? For that matter, why hadn't *I* said anything to him?!

I mean…I guess I didn't say anything be-cause…well, because I was so caught off guard and blown away by that crazy moment we shared. But wait…was it truly something we *both* felt and shared? Was it even remotely possible that Soulful Guy had felt as gobsmacked by me as I had by him? Is that even conceivable?

Wow…I knew I needed to slow down a minute and remember that I didn't exactly have a winning track record of inspiring fiery responses in men, as my friendzone mayorship proved. Surely I was once again projecting what I wanted on a situation rather than seeing things for what they truly were, like I did with the nasty case of Chad-vision I'd had for so long.

Yeah, so...probably the idea of that moment being mutual was a product of my extremely fertile imagination. However, what if I just pretended—just for fun and just for a minute or two—that it was real? That two strangers had done nothing more than see each other for a few precious seconds, and the chemistry had been immediate and blistering and one-hundred percent mutual, yet neither said a word. What kind of story would *that* be? Which romance trope? What might their conflict be?

I closed my eyes and tried to flip through the possibilities. *Hmm...well, maybe one of them is already married or has a significant other. Or one of them is kind of down and dispirited, like I was feeling when it happened. Perhaps even broken or shy. Or caught up in some dangerous situation...and the only reason they didn't say anything was to protect the other person!*

I liked the thought of that, and I tossed around the idea of writing a romantic suspense or romantic adventure story for a while. I even considered Mafia or military storylines. But in the end, as romantic as that notion was—the idea of a character based on Soulful Guy staying silent because he was madly attracted to me...er, the female protagonist...but wanted to protect her from danger—none of those angles really felt right for me.

Everyone always says that writers should "write what you know." But, like I said before, I couldn't exactly draw on personal romantic successes here. What I did know about was romance *books,* mainly because I've read so many. I've also tried out a whole lot of genres and spice levels in my reading. So I might not have a ton of personal experience with love to draw from, but I definitely know what I like to read. My absolute favorite has always been the "best friend's older brother" trope, for obvious reasons. But that didn't fit the chemistry-at-first-glance idea I was playing with, plus the Chad-scab had barely started healing. No need to rip it off so soon after.... Well, anyway, I abandoned that idea. I also love grumpy / sunshine books. That one could definitely work. Maybe Soulful Guy's character is just a grump. Or a recluse. *Hmm, maybe....*

I let my mind continue to wander, choosing tropes, considering them, and either dismissing them or throwing them on my maybe-pile. Enemies-to-lovers didn't fit. Neither did friends-to-lovers. Or bikers. What about rock stars?

I sat straight up, my eyes flying open wide as it hit me. Rock star! Yes! Even as that particular lightbulb was turning on in my brain, Claire's earlier words came back to me. I had said something about not being attracted to man-buns, and she said, *You know I'm not talking about the sexy rock star tattoo guy.*

Jake *totally* looked like a rock star; Claire was so right. And I had even thought that Soulful Guy looked familiar when I saw him…maybe they're both rock stars! And maybe the reason he didn't say anything to me was because he was afraid I was a stalker fan or a member of the paparazzi or something!

I leaned back again on the couch, smiling crazily at the ceiling as my brain continued to bat the idea around. I was pretty sure that this was it: I had my non-pantser-life story idea.

And possibly a crush on a rock star.

Chapter 16

Starting the Story

IT WAS LATE, and I really should have let the rock star idea percolate in my brain while I got some much-needed sleep. But once that idea came to me, I couldn't let it go or turn off the plot ideas that were scrolling by at dizzying speeds. Despite how aggressively my bed was calling my name, I decided to begin work on the outline. I was afraid if I didn't start typing everything out, I'd lose the inspiration by morning and my chance would be gone.

So that's how I ended up at my laptop all night—wildly jotting out details for the only story outline I'd ever created. First, I needed to write out my basic story idea so I could get a feel for the characters and the conflict. I took a deep breath, trying to collect the essence of it out of the wispy, half-formed concepts still wafting around me. Then I finally settled my fingers on the keyboard—

Rose and Jaxon spot each other in the lobby of her building. Crazy chemistry ignites in that single glance, but he's a rock star who's burned out and quickly losing himself in his fast-paced life. He's trying to step away from the spotlight for his own mental health before the next long and arduous world tour starts. In doing so, he is holing up in a random apartment where no one would think to find him. If he's going to decompress, he can't let anyone know who or where he is, including this beautiful woman who lit a fire in his weary soul through a single glance. Rose, meanwhile, just went through a devastating breakup with a man she'd always believed was her soulmate. He cheated on her, shattering both her heart and her confidence. How can she trust anyone again—even the gorgeous man who has suddenly reached deep into her heart with a single, soulful gaze?

Yes! That story idea instantly had cartoon hearts floating around my head. I liked it. No, I *loved* it. More importantly, I would totally read it. And the really good news is that if *I* would read it, surely other romance fans would as well.

There. I felt like I'd accomplished something monumental…and yet I knew that wasn't exactly true. In actuality, I hadn't really gotten anywhere yet. That was merely the seed of a story idea. It was a summary or a blurb or something, but not an outline.

That thought sent me on a long tangent of online investigation to see how other non-pantser authors—called *plotters* because they plot out their story details—create outlines. I lost track of the time I spent diving down into that particular rabbit hole. But, it turns out, basically no two authors do it the same way.

So I guessed that I simply had to figure out what would work for me. I thought about my previous writing efforts. My inspiration had always come directly from meeting or observing new people. I love that moment of introduction, when no one has preconceived notions and slates are clean. And I adore getting to fill up the blank canvas as I start to learn about their lives. Absolutely that's what draws me in—people. Their lives.

Okay, okay, this could work. I simply had to start at the same point here and figure out backstories for Rose and Jaxon; as I said, I need to begin painting the canvas of their lives. Surely that would be the perfect fire starter for my creativity.

So…yes, it was exactly that: a fire starter. Ideas about Rose and Jaxon poured out of me, and that morphed into figuring out her family and friends, and his family and bandmates. And those ideas led to possibilities for story events, plus ways to bring Rose and Jaxon together. And, of course, how to keep them apart, too.

I don't know when sleep finally caught up to me, but it did. I woke up on the couch with the laptop wedged between my cheek and the cushion. I yawned and stretched, my body aching and protesting the awkward position I'd forced on it, even as my brain caught up to the fact that my phone was ringing. I glanced at the screen even though it was almost certainly one of my parents. No one else in my life still made phone calls. Or would be awake on a Sunday morning, for that matter.

"Hey, Mom," I said, trying to sound chipper. But my voice came out in a croaking half-whisper. *Oof, should have gotten more sleep.*

"Lily! What's wrong?" she asked, starting in on me immediately. My mother is a champion worrier. "Are you sick? Haven't you been getting enough Vitamin C? I told you to start taking it, didn't I? You need to keep up your immunity, especially since you're working in that doctor's office! Heaven knows what kinds of germs you get exposed to every day!"

"Mom, relax," I said, sitting up. I wished I'd had a chance to go to the bathroom before having to deal with my mom's latest lovestorm. I know her; this could last a while. "You're the first person I've spoken to today, and my voice just isn't awake yet."

"Don't try to distract me," she countered. "Answer me: Are you taking care of yourself?"

"Yes, of course I am. And I work at a dentist's office, by the way, not a contagious disease factory."

"That's even worse!" she somehow reasoned. "All those open mouths spitting germs and bacteria everywhere!"

"So what are *you* guys up to this morning?" I asked, trying again to divert her attention off my health—which, for the record, was *not* currently being enhanced by large intakes of Vitamin C. A fact I had no intention of divulging.

"Well, your father wants to go golfing," she said, "but I just don't know. I've been trying to talk him out of it. It's going to be so hot here today, and you know how terrible he is about using sunscreen and staying hydrated."

My parents retired to Florida several years ago. My dad is constantly golfing, and my mom is constantly fretting about the weather, as though the heat index of Florida was a surprise every day.

"Is he there?" I asked. "I'd like to say hi. Can you put him on the phone?"

"Sure, honey, hang on...."

I could hear her calling his name, then the rustling of the phone being handed to him. *She's not taking good care of herself, Roger,* I heard her saying, *but she won't listen to me!* Seriously, she can be utterly relentless.

"Dad?"

"Liligator! How's my girl?"

"I'm good, Dad," I said. "Try to convince Mom I'm fine, too. Nothing's wrong, and there's absolutely nothing for her to worry about. Actually, things are pretty great."

"Well, that's good to hear," he said. I could hear him pull the phone from his ear and try to muffle it with his hand as he called, "Margaret, she's *fine!*" I laughed and rolled my eyes. Those two are hilarious. "So what's got you so happy?" he asked as soon as he returned his attention to me.

"I've got a new…well, writing buddy? I guess?" I said, suddenly unsure of how to categorize Cruz's place in my life. "He gave me some great advice. His encouragement already has me rolling with a story idea that I'm so excited about. I think I'm finally going to be able to write a book like I've always dreamed."

"If anyone can do it, it's you, honey," my dad said.

I smiled. Sure, he's my dad, so of course he thinks I can do it. But, well, Cruz's advice has me in a place where suddenly it's not feeling like a crazy dream or pointless hobby.

Which meant…well, maybe I was starting to truly believe that I could do it, too.

Chapter 17

Inner Resolve

REMEMBER THOSE hamsters I talked about? The ones that are constantly running in my head, fueled by self-doubt, anxiety, and general misery? Yeah, well, they were at it again that night after Lily first texted me. I was everywhere all at once, mentally and emotionally. Some of me was as excited and happy as I could ever remember. After all, I was chatting with Lily! *Me!* I had her number, plus I had an opportunity to get to know her better and help her with something. And maybe even become *friends* with her. It was more than I could have ever realistically hoped would happen, like a dream come true.

But it was also a nightmare in some ways, too. I was thinking what a mess my life had become and how pathetic it was that the thought of simply running into her in the hallway made me break into a cold sweat.

Jake's suggestions for how I should start working on myself were zinging around my mind too, right along with their friends, skepticism and fear. I mean, really, why would any of those things help now, when years of my mom pushing me into countless therapies and exercises didn't do a thing? Let's face it—all of it probably contributed in some way to my eventual and utterly complete meltdown.

And, of course, I was still troubled because I didn't know what I could offer to Lily as my "rut"—the issue she could help me solve. How much of a freak would she think I was if I confessed that I needed to practice things like ordering food in person rather than through an app? She definitely wouldn't see me as rugged and strong and alpha male or whatever it is she was looking for in a guy.

That was a long explanation, but it was also a really long night. I couldn't sleep because I couldn't resolve any of that or begin to let it go. So the doubts, worries, questions, and fears pummeled me like a space explorer caught in an asteroid field.

I must have eventually nodded off, though, because the next thing I knew I was startled awake by another text. The thought that it might be from Lily had me instantly grabbing for my phone before my brain had even caught up to what was happening or why I was still on the couch.

Jake: Bro, why aren't you at the gym? Ooh, tell me you're with your girl!

Me: No, but we did text each other. I told her I'm not a writer, but now I need to come up with something she can help me with.

Jake: Insert inappropriate yet totally hilarious joke here.

Me: Dude, come on, be serious. I need an idea.

Jake: Well, since you're Mr. Honesty and didn't back up my story about being a writer, I guess you should just give her some version of the truth. You're working on social skills, social anxiety, fear of leaving the house...something like that.

Me: I mean...I guess? I might freak her out.

Jake: Remember, she's already into you.

Me: Yeah, right. I don't know. I'll think about that some more.

Jake: Why don't you think about it while you're walking to the gym?

Me: Nah. Not today. I didn't get much sleep last night.

Jake: Insert another inappropriate joke.

Me: Bye, Jake.

I wasn't lying, I thought as I tossed the phone aside. It was true that I was exhausted, yeah. But…well, the whole truth was that now I was even more nervous than ever to leave my apartment. What if I ran into her? She'd walked right by me in the past a few times, sometimes looking at her phone or talking with her friend or carrying laundry or packages or whatever. Those near-encounters had been infrequent and, somehow, never brought us face to face until yesterday. So while I'd seen her plenty, she'd always been busy or distracted and never really tuned in on me. But after…well, I think she'd notice me now.

That was a whole other thing that had me amped up. I seriously didn't know what to think about that long gaze we'd shared. It just didn't make any sense to me because, in order *for* it to make sense, she would have had to be feeling the very same crackling chemistry I always experienced with her. But there's no way it could have been mutual…right? How could she possibly be dazzled by simply locking eyes with me when no one else in the world even *sees* me? It absolutely couldn't be true, and yet…. Okay, I admit that is exactly how it had sort of *seemed* at the time: like some sort of mutual bewitching. But no, it wasn't. I mean come on…it's just too crazy to even consider.

I scrubbed my hands over my face and closed my eyes. Despite how improbable it was, a part of me desperately wanted to pretend it really was a red-hot attraction that we both felt. Could I let myself forget all my usual doubts, even for a minute? I shut my eyes more tightly and let my mind conjure up the gaze again, this time allowing myself to view it as a mutually felt zap of pure attraction. The vision was so tantalizing that it almost hurt to think about. I wanted it to be real *so* badly.

I opened my eyes again, but the longing stayed with me, filling me with unfamiliar feelings like hope and possibility. A sudden strength I didn't know I possessed surged in my chest, and I knew in that moment that I had to fight for even the tiniest chance that she might feel something for me one day. In order to do that, I had to work to quell the doubts in my head. She was worth the chance and all the effort it would take. Because if there was even the smallest iota of hope that she could feel it too, I had to do exactly what Jake said and get to work on myself immediately.

Step one? I guess I'd just come out and admit to Lily that the rut I was in was one filled with social anxiety, and then I'd have to hope she'd understand. Despite everything, I really did want to change. I wanted to be someone good enough for her.

I wanted...Lily.

Chapter 18

Pure Happiness

BY THE TIME Lily started texting me that evening, I had found my inner resolve, then freaked out and talked myself out of it, about a million times. The two warring sides were battling an epic swordfight in my mind—I can do this...no I can't...back and forth they lunged and parried all day long. Mix in the lack of sleep, and I was a total wreck when my phone alerted me about her incoming text.

Lily: Hey, is now a good time to continue our chat?

Me: It's perfect.

In reality, it was terrible timing. But the allure of talking with her again was stronger than any mental battle could ever be. And that's a strong statement considering I was currently a fly trapped in anxiety's web.

Lily: Yay, because I have great news!

Me: You do? I'm intrigued....

Lily: I do, and it totally warrants intrigue! Last night I took your advice and chose a story idea to outline.

Me: Huh.

Lily: Oh no! You're underwhelmed?

Me: You do know what intrigue means, right?

I don't know what came over me in that response or how I so quickly felt free to tease Lily. After all, we barely knew each other. But there was something so *easy* about texting her. I mean…it's the way I had always been with Jake—joking and goofing on him all the time. But no one else had ever brought out that side of me before. I tried not to overthink it too much and just roll with it since she seemed to be joking with me, too.

Lily: Come on, admit that you're still intrigued and want to hear more!

Me: Of course, just teasing. You've got an outline already? Wow, is the process normally that fast? I don't know how this stuff works.

Lily: Nah, it's not that fast, but I did come up with an awesome story idea! I'm totally inspired now.

Me: Whoa, that's great! Congratulations!

Lily: Thank you! Thank you twice, I guess. You were the one who started me down the right path.

Me: I feel like I didn't really do anything, but you're welcome.

Lily: No, seriously, you did a lot! Wanna hear the idea?

Me: Of course.

Lily: Okay. It's going to be a rock star romance with a hidden-identity trope!

Me: Er…

Lily: Tropes are common story plots or themes. They set up certain expectations for the readers. Try to keep up, Cruz! (;

Me: Gah, sorry. Go on…

Lily: Okay, so, my main characters are Rose, who's coming off a painful breakup, and Jaxon, who's a burned-out rock star. Still with me?

Me: No fancy words, so yes.

Lily: Good. Okay, so their meet-cute is…wait, do you know what a meet-cute is?

Me: Does it help that I wish I did?

Lily: You're so high maintenance! Okay, so a meet-cute is the big scene where they meet for the first time. Although this isn't going to be a rom com, so I guess it really wouldn't technically be...you know what, never mind. So, they meet...

Me: ...and it's cute. See? I can learn things.

Lily: Lol. Okay, so he's hiding out in a nowheresville apartment where no one would ever dream they'd find a rock star. He's just trying to lay low.

Me: Why wouldn't he just go rent an island or a penthouse or something?

Lily: Oof. Thaaaanks Cruz. Yeah, that's totally a plot hole, isn't it? Ugh, I don't know. I'll have to think about that.

Me: Sorry, picking things apart is a specialty of mine.):

Lily: No are you crazy? That's exactly the kind of feedback I need! But do you want to hear about how they meet or what?

Me: Yes, edge of my seat!

Lily: That's more like it. Okay, so he's in this dumpy apartment building for...reasons, and she lives there because she's an everyday, average person. Do you see any more problems?

Me: Yeah, are these two ever going to meet or what?

Lily: Lol, so impatient! Okay, so she's in the lobby of her building, and she's had a crappy day because of the breakup and everything. She's upset and worried and sad, and absolutely everything sucks...until she sees Jaxon.

Me: Ooh! Reaching for popcorn....

Lily: I know, right? So she sees him, and Jaxon sees her, and like...the world just stops in that instant for both of them. They're completely lost in each other's eyes, their worries melt away, and the chemistry sizzles palpably in the air. The two of them, in a single glance, have created pure, heart-stopping magic.

My eyes were comically wide as the phone slid right out of my hand. I stared at it where it landed at my feet as the synapses in my head wildly tried to process her words and catch up to the automatic physical reaction I was having. That scene...what she'd just described...was *us!* Lily had recounted what had happened between *us!* I was...floored, flabbergasted, blown away. All those things were wrapped up together in an avalanche of surprise that was hurtling its way through me.

I tried to pull myself together as I leaned over and picked up the phone, as though the precious words it held might shatter like glass. I took a shaky breath and painstakingly re-read her description.

Wow, she...she had felt it too.

There was no other way to interpret it, right? I read her words over and over until they were etched into my soul, and then I read them again. Surely there couldn't be any other way to interpret it: *She really had felt it too.* "Pure, heart-stopping magic," is how she'd described it. Yeah, *exactly!* That's what it had felt like for me too. My heart started to beat faster, and I could feel happiness fireworks begin to explode in my chest.

Lily: You still there? You hated it, didn't you? Too unbelievable? More plot holes? Were they more like plot craters?

Me: Sorry! I dropped my phone. No, it was the opposite...I loved it.

I could hear a high-pitched squeal of excitement easily cutting its way through our thin walls. I'd almost forgotten that we were neighbors, and that Lily was very likely writing those words to me from such a close distance. Somehow it made the moment even more astonishing for me. Lily was right there on the other side of that wall... *writing about me!*

Lily: Freaking out here! I love that you love it!

Me: I do. I mean, I'm not your typical romance reader, but I think it sounds great. What happens next?

Lily: Well, like I said, I don't have the whole outline. They're both going to feel a longing for each other, but her recent heartbreak and trust issues will hold her back. Meanwhile, his desire for anonymity and not knowing if she's a groupie will hold him back.

Me: It sounds like a great story, Lily. Really.

Lily: Squee!

I don't know where the burst of bravery came from in my next response, I really don't. But suddenly I absolutely had to find out more.

Me: Is this based on a true story? Are you heartbroken? Or...wait, are you the rock star?!

Lily: Ha! No, not a rock star. And no true breakup backstory. But...okay, truth time. Yeah, it's somewhat based on a recent experience I had.

For the first time in as long as I could remember, a smile of pure happiness dawned on my face.

Chapter 19

Trying to Be Subtle

I DON'T KNOW WHY I was so excited that Cruz liked my story idea. I mean, I actually squealed like a little girl when he responded positively about it. But, well, I guess since he was the first person I'd mentioned it to, the fact that he seemed to love it felt important.

Cruz: Okay, now I'm really intrigued. Tell me about this recent experience.

Me: Uh…I don't know.

Cruz: Sorry, too personal?

Me: It's not that. I just…I'm not sure how to process it fully, I guess. And besides, I've just been blabbing about ME this whole time anyway. You know, you never did tell me why Jake thought I could help you.

Cruz: Oh yeah, that.

Me: Tapping foot impatiently….

Cruz: Okay, okay. You know I told you I'm a web designer?

Me: Yeah.

Cruz: I do it freelance from home. I do all my transactions from home, actually.

Me: Okay…?

Cruz: So that means, you know, I order my groceries online. I use apps for food delivery. I shop for clothes online. Other than the gym, I basically never have to go anywhere.

Me: You just described everyone, everywhere.

Cruz: Right, but it's more than that.

Me: Huh? Jake wanted you to work on a project, right? I'm not following how this relates to that.

Cruz: I'm getting there. Geez, the impatience!

Me: I'm totally not impatient. But would you tell me already?! (;

Cruz: Okay, okay! It's just that somewhere along the way I didn't merely lose the desire to go out of the house and have normal transactions...I, well, I'm kind of losing the ability altogether.

Me: Whoa, back this train up...you're agoraphobic?

Cruz: Well, no. I'm not afraid to leave the house or anything. Like I said, I go to the gym. But Jake worries I'm losing touch with the outside world and my ability to interact with it.

Me: Ohhh.

Cruz: So I think when he met you and heard you talking about needing a buddy or partner or whatever, he thought that I could use one, too.

I smiled dreamily to my living room as my thoughts sprang back to that meeting with Jake...and Soulful Guy. Maybe this was my opportunity to learn more about him from Cruz. I decided right then to try my hand at some subtle prying.

Me: That makes sense, I guess. I'd be happy to help you with that project! My secret superpower is talking to people, you know.

Cruz: Good, cuz it's my kryptonite.

Me: I've got this! And so will you!

Cruz: I hope so. That would be great, actually.

Me: Yes! We'll hatch an entire step-by-step plan

to get you out into the world and release your inner social butterfly.

Cruz: That sounds ambitious. But great, too. Thanks Lily.

Me: Of course! It's the least I could do after you helped me already. So, before we start coming up with that plan, I have a question. Did Jake say anything else about that day? You know…like maybe who he was with, for example?

Okay, so subtlety wasn't one of my stronger gifts. Still, I was dying to find out what Cruz might know about Soulful Guy, so I needed to get to the point.

Cruz: All he said about it was that you were hot. And that I should reply if you texted me.

Jake thought *I* was hot? *Jake?!* With his muscles and man-bun and hot-guy swagger? *That* guy thought I, Lily of the Friendzone, was hot?

Okay, I admit it, that had me squealing again.

Me: Shut up! He did not say I was hot!

There was a long pause before Cruz replied. I could see the dots indicating that he was working on one, but the longer it took, the more embarrassed I was getting. He was probably trying to find a nice way to tell me that, duh, he was just being polite. A guy like Jake would never find my girl-next-door vibe appealing. No way. And seriously, what did it matter? It wasn't Jake I was attracted to that day anyway.

Just as I was starting to type out an apology and a retraction, his reply finally arrived—

Cruz: Lily, is Jake your rock star? Is he the one who you felt you created magic with?

Nope—he was way off-base. But since my efforts at stealth had been so pathetic, I figured I'd better stop while I was somewhat ahead. I was already dying of embarrassment; I didn't need to invite any more of it into the conversation by confessing the huge crush I was quickly developing on a complete stranger. I'd have to find Soulful Guy on my own, it seemed. And pray that he actually lived in this building so I *could* find him.

Me: Ha! Who's impatient now?! Like I'd confess that on only our second text-date!

Again, Cruz was slow to respond. *Maybe he's busy or distracted or something,* I thought, as I nudged him with another reply.

Me: You still there?

Cruz: Hey, can we chat tomorrow? I've got to go.

Me: Um, sure....

I exhaled slowly as I did a quick review of our conversation. It had clearly ended uncomfortably and abruptly, and I wasn't sure why. Did I weird him out by saying we were on a text-date? Did the possibility of me crushing on Jake make Cruz feel like I was just using him to get to Jake? Had I been joking around too much when he was trying to open up to me about his social anxieties? Had I unwittingly fed into those anxieties?

I wasn't sure exactly how I'd messed up, but I certainly felt unsettled with the way we'd left things. Plus, I hadn't gotten anywhere with finding out about Soulful Guy.

Restless energy thrummed through me, and I wasn't sure how to fix things. I didn't really know Cruz well enough to just text or call him right back and ask him outright. Eventually I decided to give him some space while I channeled my embarrassment and regret into coming up with some ideas that might help him.

I may not have answers for almost any other area of my life, but meeting and talking with people? *That* I knew how to do.

Chapter 20

The Welfare Check

OF *COURSE* Lily had been attracted to Jake. *He* was her rock star, not me. After all, Jake was…well, Jake. Muscles, confidence, charisma, the whole rock star package. And I, of course, was still me. Anxious. Closed down. And entirely unable to just march next door and ask Lily out….

The more I thought about it—and this was *me* we're talking about, so naturally I'd been obsessing about it with the kind of laser focus that brain surgeons require—the more hopeless I felt about it. It was such a joke that I'd worked myself into believing she had felt the same chemistry between us that day. What in the world would someone as bubbly and wonderful as Lily possibly see in a guy as broken as me?

Nothing.

So, yeah, I was in a full-on spiral. Not good since it was Monday and I had countless projects in various stages of development that I needed to complete.

My phone chimed with an incoming text. My heart leapt, still foolishly wanting to hear more from Lily despite the emotional blow it had taken when I realized it was Jake who she liked.

Speaking of Jake, it was his name, and not Lily's, that I saw pop up on the screen. Even in the midst of my spiral, I felt disappointed. Apparently I still wanted to hear from her, crush on my brother notwithstanding.

Jake: Day Two and still no Max at the gym. What gives?

Me: I'm busy.

Jake: Nope! Not happening. You either get over here or I'll be showing up at your door.

Me: Jake, seriously, I'm fine. You don't need to worry about me all the time.

Jake: Yeah, actually I do. What's going on bro? Last I heard, you were chatting with your hot neighbor and promising to work on yourself. Now suddenly you're hiding from me and apparently regressing. Did she shut you down?

Me: I can't talk about this with you.

Jake: Exactly who will you talk about it with then? Mitch? Mom?

Me: No and no.

Jake: So, come on, what gives? Did she tell you to get lost? Is that it? Or maybe you're realizing she's not as perfect as you built her up to be?

Me: No, it's not that. She's better than I ever dreamed, and trust me, I'd already imagined she was pretty great.

Jake: Maxwell, come on. Talk to me.

Me: Seriously, it's nothing. Just go lift heavy things and stop fussing over me like an old woman.

Jake: See you soon...

Me: What? No! Lily might see you!

There was no reply to that, so I tried calling, but he didn't pick up. Frustration surged in me, both with Jake and with myself. If I wasn't such a mess, two days away from the gym wouldn't trigger a welfare check. It was yet another reminder of how far I'd fallen.

By the time Jake arrived, though, I knew the coast

was probably clear and that they wouldn't likely run into each other in the hall or something. The sound of Lily's door closing earlier told me she was leaving around her usual time.

"You look like you got run over by a dump truck," was Jake's cheerful greeting as he noisily pushed into the room and started his critical assessment of me. "Talk. To. Me."

I rolled my eyes and shook my head. He could be such a pit bull.

"L-leave it alone," I said. "N-nothing's wrong. I gave her advice about wr-writing, and it seemed to h-help."

"Okay, great!" he said, pride lighting his face. "I knew this would be good. What did you tell her about yourself? Last time we talked, you told me you'd already owned up that you aren't a writer."

"Yeah," I said, nodding as I took a seat at my table. "Coffee?"

"No thanks, and don't try to distract me," he said as he invited himself into the seat across from me. "Talk!"

"I told her that w-working from home had made m-me start losing touch with r-reality," I said. "That I'm l-losing social skills."

"Not a lie," he said. "That's good."

"Yeah. She s-said she'd be happy to h-help."

"Maxwell, that pretty angel of yours knows about your anxieties and wants to help you," my brother replied with a distinct note of confusion. "What in the world has you up in your head about that?"

I closed my eyes, feeling embarrassed and filled with regret that I had to confess everything to him. But since he wasn't going to give up until he got the entire story, I decided I may as well just put it out there.

"I th-think she's into *you,*" I said, the words crackling out of my throat.

"Dude, no way!" he said, instantly shaking his head. "You forget that I was there that day. Bro, she didn't even *look* at me twice! She couldn't see me clearly, because the minute her big blue eyes saw you, those little emoji hearts were suddenly floating in front of them, blocking her view."

"Shut up," I said, although I couldn't stop a little half smile from turning up the corners of my mouth. "I mean, yeah, that's what I thought happened, too. That's what I *wished* had happened, anyway. But her texts were pretty clear. It's you she's thinking about."

"Show me," he demanded, the disbelief clear on his face. "I think you're interpreting something the wrong way. It makes sense, really. Your confidence has been circling the drain for so long that you don't know up from down anymore."

It felt like I was betraying Lily's confidence by sharing the texts but…well, Jake wasn't wrong. My issues had issues of their own. Maybe I wasn't seeing things the right way? How would I ever know if I didn't let him help me? So I pulled up the text chain with Lily, rolled it back to the start, and handed it over to him.

He read it like he was studying for a critical exam while I watched, amazed for the billionth time by what a great brother he was. How many of them would do this sort of thing? How many would have even sensed something was bugging me in the first place?

He chuckled a few times, a smile creasing his face. Then he said, "Maxwell, so far I don't see a single thing to worry about. And actually, this is giving me a ton of hope. You're being your real, awesome self with her.

You're opening up to her. This is perfect!"

"Yeah, I thought so too, but...just keep reading."

So he did exactly that until I could see he'd come to the end, when I'd cut off our contact last night. I fully expected him to shrug and admit that yeah, there was something to what I was seeing, so I couldn't have been more shocked when he lifted his head up to reveal a big sloppy grin on his face.

"Duuude!" he said triumphantly. "I was so right. I am a matchmaking *genius*. She is so into you that she can't contain the feelings. She's writing a story about *you*, bro!"

"Huh?!" I replied, thoroughly perplexed. "That's n-not what I s-see at all!"

"Max, look at the evidence! In her story, she describes that eyeball thing you two did in the lobby, right?"

"That's what I th-thought at f-first, sure," I conceded. "But—"

"But nothing!" he said, cutting me off. "Then she tried to get you to cough up information about *you*. She said...." He trailed off as he hunted through the texts. "Oh, okay. Here it is. She said: *Did Jake say anything else about that day? You know...like maybe who he was with, for example?* It's right there! *That's* your proof! Stop creating problems where there aren't any. Maxwell, listen to me. This girl is totally into you! But instead of giving her a break and dropping some clues about *you*—the guy she obviously wants to know more about—you decided to light your opportunity on fire and tell her that I thought she was hot. Why would you even say that?!"

"B-because I'm an idiot? B-but I could h-hear her shriek about it th-through the wall," I said. "She f-freaked out at even the th-thought of you b-being into her."

"Nah, chill out," he said. "Everyone likes the thought of someone being attracted to them. Wouldn't it make you feel good if you knew her friend had thought *you* were hot that day?"

I shrugged.

"You would. *Anyone* would. It's a normal human emotion. Max, I've been around enough women both at the gym and on photoshoots, and I've dated enough of them, to have a basic feel for whether or not they're attracted to me. Look me in the eye and hear me right now. I'm *not* lying to you. This is not a trick to get you to come out of your shell. I swear to you right now that she was not even looking at me that day. Her cute little question about whether I mentioned anyone else confirms it. She was digging for information about *you,* and then she got embarrassed when you were being so dense about it."

I did look him in the eye, read the sincerity on his face, and worked to match those things up with my memories of that day along with the words she'd texted. As all of that evidence mixed together in my mind, some of the doubt finally started to loosen its grip on me and melt away.

Maybe, just maybe, he was right.

Chapter 21

Moving to California

Lily: Cruz, I hope now is an okay time to talk, because I've been feeling like such a jerk all day about our last chat. Here you were confiding in me about something you'd like some help with, and I was being insensitive and joking around and trying to get info out of you…. I guess I just wanted to apologize to you. I'm sorry!

The arrival of Lily's text jerked me awake. Apparently, I'd fallen asleep at my desk at some point. That was the second time in as many days that I'd fallen asleep in an awkward spot, only to be awakened by an incoming text.

I think the lack of sleep was starting to take a toll. Although after Jake left that morning, I'd felt so much better about—well, *everything*—that I was finally able to dive into some of the work that'd been stacking up. But since I'd gotten such terrible sleep since the day I saw Lily in the lobby, it hadn't taken much for me to nod off on my laptop.

I read her words and was instantly filled with remorse. I was so quick to shut her down when I thought she liked Jake, and that was so stupid of me. For one thing, Lily's clearly a great person, and I seriously doubt she'd try to hurt me on purpose even if she did know about this lie I was perpetrating. But on top of that, the friendship we'd started cultivating between us shouldn't hinge on whether or not she was attracted to me. I mean really, who am I to be walking away from potential friendships or attaching strings to them? I needed all the friends I could get, and the whole truth of the matter was that I wanted Lily in my life, regardless of whether or not it was in a romantic way.

Me: Whoa, no—you didn't do or say anything wrong. That was all on me for ending the chat awkwardly. I'm sorry. I guess I got distracted last night. See? I told you I wasn't good at social interactions....

Lily: You're sure? We're good?

Me: We're more than good.

Lily: So...great, then?

Me: Lol, yes. Great > good.

Lily: Ooh, math nerd! I like it.

Me: Nerd, yes. Math, no.

Lily: Well, nerd, you're in luck! Because I'm ready for us to come up with a plan to help you.

Me: Okay.... You're sure about this? Honestly, I'm totally embarrassed.

Lily: Oh, come on. Isn't helping each other what our partnership is all about?

Me: Yeah, I guess so.

Lily: Listen, after we talk this out, if you're still feeling embarrassed, I'll tell you something ridiculously embarrassing that happened to me recently. Deal?

Me: Lol. Okay, deal. So do you already have some ideas for me to try?

Lily: Yeah...but first, what have you tried so far?

Me: I've tried...sitting in my living room and rarely

leaving except to go to the gym....

Lily: Gee, that hasn't worked? Huh, well I guess I'll cross that off my imaginary list of terrible ideas....

Me: Lol.

Lily: So you're telling me you've never tried anything?

Me: ....

Lily: Okay, have you ever THOUGHT about trying anything?

Me: Yeah. Well, Jake suggested practicing things like going shopping in person. Buying my own groceries. And no longer doing everything online.

Lily: Yeah, that's kind of what I was thinking, too. Oooh! I could go with you the first time! Wanna get coffees or something?! Do you live somewhere nearby?

Me: No. California.

Lily: What?! You live in California? I guess this whole time I just assumed you were local, like Jake. Wait...you said you're free in the evenings, but there's a time difference. You didn't mention that before.

Me: Oh, yeah, no big deal. #freelancerlife

Yeah, okay, so I choked. The minute Lily suggested accompanying me on my first attempt at socializing myself like a feral cat, I completely freaked out. I tossed out Mitch's location before I could even really think about whether or not I wanted to be lying to her. One second of panic and *blam!*—I'd moved to California. I never even thought about the time difference.

Lily: Well, there goes my coffee idea. Should we rope one of your local friends into going, then?

I'd lied about California, but should I lie about my

complete lack of friends? I mean…I had Jake. And now there was Lily…well, sort of. So, hey, in the past few days, I'd doubled my number of friends. That was progress, right?

I considered lying again, the way I'd so easily rolled out that California thing. But I already felt miserably guilty about it. So I didn't—

Me: Honestly, I'm a bit of a hermit.

Lily: No local friends?

Me: The struggle is real.

Lily: Huh. But wait, how do you know Jake?

Me: We grew up together.

Lily: Oh nice, like Claire and me. Is he originally from out there, or are you from here?

Me: I grew up in Jersey.

Lily: Okay, so you moved out to California, started working a home-based job, and never made friends in the new location? Wait, why did you move there if you can work from anywhere?

Now I was *really* panicking. In the span of about a minute, she'd poked countless holes in my terrible cover story. Now I had to come up with a motivation for having moved. I didn't want to keep lying to her, but I'd already dug this hole, so I decided I may as well get a bigger shovel and keep going.

My mind wandered to Mitch. Why had *he* moved out there? At the time, he'd floated a vaguely flimsy story about wanting to "be where the action was," but honestly, it had never rung true to me. He'd seemed so angry all the time, and that's how he'd been for years. I understood it though, even as a little kid. I'd dealt with my dad by completely shutting down. Jake had been the peacekeeper, trying to keep everyone calm while stepping in as my protector, friend, parent, and all-around lifeline. But Mitch? Mitch got *mad*. Mad at everyone and everything, I guess: our dad, our mom, the situation, and maybe even me. I think at some point he just couldn't take it anymore, and the next thing any of us knew, he was across the country. I'd always wondered if he really loved California or if he'd randomly picked a place that wasn't here.

Lily: You still there?

Me: Just trying to decide how honest to be here.

Lily: Hit me, I can take it! Or...wait, am I being too nosy?

Me: Nah. It's just...okay, here's the thing: I had a rough childhood. I have always wanted to be anywhere that my dad wasn't.

Lily: Ohhh...I'm so sorry Cruz! California's making more sense now.

Me: Yeah. So here I am, and no, I don't have any friends for you to set me up with on a coffee playdate. Ugh, have I told you yet that this is embarrassing?

Lily: Aww come on, you don't have to be embarrassed! Definitely not with me. But...okaaay, I guess we're doing this. I guess it's story time.

Chapter 22

Coffee and Confessions

I DON'T KNOW why I felt able and willing to talk about the Chad fiasco with Cruz. But at some point in our conversation, I suddenly realized it was absolutely natural and right to open up with him like that. I mean, come on, here he was being so completely honest and vulnerable with me about important, personal things like a bad relationship with his dad and his social anxieties. So I became filled with the need to hand him a piece of myself equal to what he'd willingly offered to me.

Cruz: Story time?

Me: Yeah, remember? We'll be embarrassment buddies. It'll be fun.

Cruz: I find your use of the word "fun" suspicious.

Me: Uh, well, I'm using an older definition.

Cruz: Back when it meant "not fun"?

Me: Exactly. Now shut up. Do you want to hear my embarrassing story or what?

Cruz: Hit me.

Me: Okay, so, my best friend Claire has an older brother, Chad.

Cruz: Hate him already.

Me: Lol. Yes! Keep that energy. So, I've always had a crush on him. Like...a big-time, thought-we'd-be-together-forever kind of crush. Have you ever had one of those?

Cruz: Yeah.

Me: Good, then you get my general headspace here. I crushed on him for YEARS! Like, since I was nine. But recently Claire suggested me as a date for some work event he had to go to, and he was completely grossed out at the thought.

Cruz: Have I mentioned I hate Chad?

Me: Right? He said I'm annoying and I never shut up. He said dating me would be "like dating Tinkerbell riding a unicorn," and then he called me Silly Lily.

Cruz: I....????

Me: Yeah. Are you laughing at me? I can't believe I just blurted all of that out to you. It happened kind of recently, actually. I'm still really upset about it.

Cruz: Lily, I've only known you for about five minutes so I can't tell if you're being serious right now.

Me: Trust me, I wouldn't kid about this. Actually, that's what I was so down about the day I ran into Jake.

Cruz: I'm completely blown away here. You couldn't have shocked me more if you tried. I can't imagine anyone saying any of that about you. I can't even imagine anyone saying any of that NEAR you. You're funny, kind, sweet...nothing he said fits with the person I'm getting to know.

Me: Thanks, Cruz. Yes, we're in the early stages here, but that means a lot. And, FWIW, you're pretty great yourself. You'll have more friends than you know what to do with once you let people in.

Cruz: Thanks, Lily. Really. But can I say one more thing about your story?

Me: Yeah...?

Cruz: Chad's a tool.

Me: Lol. Embarrassment buddies unite!

Cruz: Definitely. Okay, so...awkwardly changing topic...you said coffee? You think my first outing should be to get coffee?

Me: Well, yeah. Unless you don't like coffee...?

Cruz: I do. It's just that I make it at home. Y'know, in a coffeepot on the kitchen counter. I don't know any of those fancy orders you see people make in shows and movies. It's like they're just saying random sounds. They're all venti splash half caf whip dip dink dork.

Me: Lol!!! You don't have to make it complicated, though. You could just order a hot coffee, black, and then dump in whatever you normally use with your sweet coffeepot setup when you get home.

Cruz: Don't diss the coffeepot! But...really? They won't think I'm a weirdo?

Me: Not about the coffee. –(;

Cruz: Funny! Okay, okay. If you're sure it can be that simple, I guess I can make asking for a black coffee my first outing.

Me: You got this! And I'll keep working on my outline. This is going to be awesome, for both of us. You'll see!

I smiled as I hit send on that last message. I couldn't believe how comfortable I already felt with Cruz, and I wasn't even sure why. Was it because his comments got me rolling on a story idea I'm so excited about? Was it because I just love meeting new people in general, and it had nothing to do with him in particular? Maybe...or maybe it was Cruz himself. He was nice, funny, kind, and not afraid to make himself vulnerable by opening up about painful topics. I mean really, what wasn't there to like?

I told him I needed to keep working on my outline, which wasn't a lie. But I also wanted to go on an outing of my own to try to find Soulful Guy. I'd been putting off laundry for a ridiculously long time and was coming up on one of those "do the laundry or buy new underwear" forks in the road. Maybe this was the perfect opportunity to start scouring the building for him.

I mean come on…even rock stars need clean laundry.

Chapter 23

The Pizza Order

I KNEW THAT Lily typically went to work early, which is when I'm usually at the gym. So I could easily walk right into Say Java the next morning after leaving the gym without fear of running into her. And although that made total sense, a huge part of me was scared that if I didn't go immediately while Lily's encouragement was still glowing inside me, I'd talk myself out of it. Then again, getting coffee at night made no sense. With the terrible sleep I'd been getting lately, the last thing I needed was a jolt of after-sundown caffeine. And if I tried to get decaf, that would complicate the order, which was also something I didn't need. Plus, I didn't think they'd be open now anyway.

I'd managed to sleep half the day away and was starving. Could I really go somewhere and place a food order in person, though? It seemed too ambitious for a first attempt since there'd be too much to say and too many questions about sides and sauces and drinks to answer. A pizza order might be simpler, I decided. *Oh...but then I'd have to stand around and wait for it to bake.* Plus, I'd be forced to interact again with someone when it came time to pay for it. That sounded excruciating.

Worrying that a pizza order was too ambitious felt like such a stupid problem to have, which instantly turned my dad's voice on at full blast in my head, where it's always lurking anyway—

We gotta get this kid tested!

Maybe he needs a special school or something!

Hazel, I'm starting to wonder if there's something seriously wrong with him!

I rolled my eyes in frustration, more with myself than with him. He had been a terrible father, yes. And certainly nothing had ever indicated that he was interested in changing that or starting over with me. I'd cut him out of my life when I moved out, not that he'd exactly been fighting to see me in the first place. But somehow, in the intervening years, I hadn't figured out how to make him pack his bags and move out of my *head* the same way I'd moved out of his house. Clearly that was part of what I needed to work on. I'd never have a full and happy life while he still had this level of power over me—and, more precisely, over my self-esteem. I was letting him stand between me and social freedom. Which meant he was also standing between me and a chance at being with Lily, something I absolutely could not accept.

That alone had me dialing the pizza place down the block from the apartment building before I even had a chance to plan what I needed to say.

"Pickup or delivery?" the voice on the other end of the line said, startling me with how quickly they had answered. I tried to ignore the shock and focus on my reply, but quick answers have never been my specialty. Apparently, I had paused too long, because the voice was soon in my ear again. "Hello?"

"H-hi…uh, p-p-p…."

"Pickup?"

"Y-yes," I said, my cheeks burning now.

"Okay," he said. "I've got the number on the caller ID. What's the name for the order?"

"M-M-Max," I managed to say despite how

flustered I was quickly becoming. As usual, the more I tried to battle my stutter, the fewer words I could manage.

"Okay, Max, what can I get ya?"

"P-p-plain," I said, even though I honestly would have liked a few toppings. Maybe someday in the future I could actually add things to the order.

"Plain cheese? Large? Anything else?"

"N-no," I said, happy that at least I had managed a definitive tone to the word. "Th-thanks."

"You got it," he said. "Give it about twenty minutes."

As I was debating whether or not to say anything else, I realized he'd disconnected the call.

*   *   *

I laid the phone down and stared at it, thinking back on the order and trying to measure my degree of success. I could look at it two different ways, I decided.

I could focus on how I'd barely been able to communicate through my jackhammering stutter. Based on that, I could then drown in the embarrassment that always comes when people helpfully try to guess what I'm saying and finish words for me, as the pizza guy had done when I couldn't say *pickup*. Then I could take the mortification even further and decide to forget all of this. Who could blame me, after all? This was too hard. Too much.

Or...I guess I could think about the fact that—hot mess of a phone call or not—a pizza was currently being assembled for me. I had successfully placed the order.

Even as those two warring views on the call unfurled in my mind, I suddenly realized it wasn't my dad's words I could currently hear in my head, but Lily's—

You got this! And I'll keep working on my outline. This is going to be awesome, for both of us. You'll see!

She'd recently suffered a huge embarrassment of her own. The words that Chad-the-jackwagon had said to her were absolutely brutal. Much harsher than someone as sweet and caring as Lily ever deserved. But had she let his words stop her even though she'd had feelings for the guy? Was she currently rocking back-and-forth in a corner or was she just brushing it off, moving on, and trying to fulfill her writing dreams? Obviously, she was choosing the second option.

Could I do the same thing?

Jake seemed to think so, and he knew all that I'd been through. Lily didn't know everything, but she seemed to have some faith in me regardless. Maybe it was time to replace my father's negativity with their positivity. *Maybe....*

I was grabbing my wallet and keys and walking out of my apartment before I could even finish that thought. I had to stay on course. It was time. Time to go pick up a pizza. Time to try.

Time...for change.

Chapter 24

Elevator Encounter

I GOT ALL THE WAY into the basement before I realized my detergent bottle was basically empty. What little was left wasn't close to enough to wash the mountain of clothes I'd just gotten done wrestling down the hallway, into the elevator, and finally the laundry room.

I debated what to do. I could take it as a sign from the laundry gods that they weren't pleased with me and just haul the pile back to my apartment for another day. Or I could roll with it and leave my basket there for a few minutes while I ran across the street to the small convenience store, which always carried all sorts of last-minute essentials. I had slung on a crossbody purse in order to pay for the coin-operated washing machines, so I could easily purchase detergent.

With a sigh and a roll of my eyes, I shoved my basket into a corner and headed for the elevator. Yes, I was only going up one floor to the lobby, but the stairwells were dark and kind of freaky, so I tended to avoid them.

The store did indeed have detergent—*Thank you laundry gods, I'm sorry I doubted you!*—and it was while I was standing at the corner waiting for the light to change that I saw him. It was Soulful Guy! Well, at least that's who it *looked* like from a distance. The guy I saw had a pizza in one hand and was opening the door that leads to the apartment building's lobby with the other.

"Wait!" I yelled, but he walked through without stopping.

Luck was with me, though, as the light changed right as the door closed behind him. I jogged across the street, detergent in hand like I was rushing toward a five-alarm laundry emergency. I tried to pick up the pace even more when I reached the other side and started down the sidewalk, praying the elevator hadn't magically gotten faster in the past ten or so minutes. I hoped I could catch him. And, well...I hoped it was really him. The short, dark hair looked right. So did his tall, muscular build. But since my glance had been so fleeting, I just wasn't sure.

Right as I clattered into the lobby, I saw him again, walking into the elevator at the far end.

I should have yelled to see if he'd hold the doors. But all I could think to say was, "Hey!" as I raced toward him, skidding to a breathy halt as they started to close.

Once again, lightning struck the moment our eyes met. I watched as recognition lit up his dark brown eyes, and I heard myself gasp as a current of awareness coursed through me. What I should have done was try to elbow my way into the closing doors, but I was frozen and dumbstruck by the feelings he could stir up in me in a mere glance. This sounds crazy, but he must have been feeling the same way, because his mouth opened as though he were about to say something but, like me, was too lost in our stare to find the words.

"What's your name?" I finally thought to ask, breaking our shocked silence right as the doors shut completely, severing the tie between us.

The elevator pinged, and I jumped forward, pushing the button over and over like a little kid. But the doors didn't open again, and I could hear the elevator lumbering its way up and away from me.

*   *   *

Dazed and frustrated, I walked to the stairwell and thumped my way down to the laundry room, my brain spinning crazily.

The chemistry between Soulful Guy and me *wasn't* something in my imagination. Yes, I had a terrible track record of getting friendzoned by guys. Yes, Chad thought I was a silly mess. And yes, the encounter at the elevator just now had been about three seconds long, tops. But I *saw* it. And I *felt* it. Plus, there was *his* reaction to seeing me again—the heat burning in his blistering gaze. I knew with absolute certainty, taking up residence in every cell in my body, that he felt it too. Everything I was experiencing when I saw him had been reflected back in his eyes. He'd been every bit as electrified and overwhelmed as I was. He was *into me!*

But, of course, I'm me, and I couldn't stop worrying and wondering and doubting. I mean, I had only recently fancied myself in love with freaking Chad, after all.

I got to the laundry room to find my mountain still there in the corner, waiting for me in judgy silence. And the machines were still open and available. As I got to work sorting my clothes into different washers, a new thought occurred: Was my brain making more of the two interactions with Soulful Guy than what was really there, simply to compensate for the Chad-pain? Was I somehow transferring those unrequited feelings onto a new victim as a means of self-preservation?

The thought was painful and embarrassing, but I let myself do a lazy backstroke through it as I analyzed it. It might have some merit, I finally decided. After all,

I'd carried my Chad-feelings around with me for years, like some kind of security blanket. It made a lot of sense that I had a void I was looking to fill.

I tried to picture and compare Chad and Soulful Guy and honestly consider my feelings for both of them. What quickly became apparent was that my reactions to them weren't equal. Chad had inspired hero worship in me. He'd been older, popular, and cool. And he'd always been helpful and kind to me—well, until Claire revealed his *true* feelings, that is. I'd always thought he was just a great all-around guy, and he made me feel sort of tingly and excited about getting to know him better. But I had never, not once, been *electrified* by him. We'd never had any mutual chemistry explosions or anything close. What I had felt for him was fun and youthful and sweet. But Soulful Guy on the other hand? We'd never even spoken, and yet the blazing-hot chemistry had shouted louder than any words possibly could.

Was it healthy to drop one crush and immediately start up another? Probably not. But was I doing it anyway?

Absolutely.

Chapter 25

Wyatt Levine

THAT PLAIN PIZZA tasted like victory. Not only had I placed an order on the phone and picked it up in person, but I'd gotten to see Lily, too—all thanks to my willingness to *try* for once.

Seeing her again felt like getting zapped by those cardiac paddles you see on medical shows, where the person holding them yells, *"Clear!"* before zapping the guy. Well, those paddles apparently did their job just fine because I could feel my heart thumping crazily in my chest at the mere memory of her adorable dash across the lobby to see me. At least it *looked* like she'd been running to catch me as she skidded to a stop while the elevator doors closed. I'd started to say something to her in return, but the usual issues with fear and nervousness had frozen the words in my throat. I'd ended up staring at her like some lovestruck mime. After two silent interactions with me, she had to be wondering what in the world my problem was. I didn't even have the chance to reply when she asked me my name. The elevator was already moving by the time "Max" worked its way out of my mouth.

Then again, I don't know what I would have done if the elevator doors *hadn't* already been closing. Would I have tried to do more than choke out my name in my typical halting manner? And would seeing me struggle to utter the most basic conversation starters have made her rethink her attraction to me? Maybe....

But maybe not. Thanks to our text conversations—which included her willingness to open up about a really painful experience—Lily's world already seemed like a safe place to me. If I was ever going to open myself up to anyone, it would definitely be her. I tried to match up what I knew about her with my fears of rejection, and the visions just didn't mesh. I didn't feel as though she was that kind of person at all. She definitely wouldn't be cruel, no. But she might very well move me into her friendzone. Being kind about someone's differences is hardly the same as being attracted in spite of them.

As I was thinking about it, a text chimed on my phone. I savored the luxury of not knowing who it might be from after so many years of hearing exclusively from Jake. But it *was* Jake, of course—

Jake: You. Me. Gym. Tomorrow.

Me: Did you hit your head and forget sentences?

Jake: Funny. But I'm serious.

Me: I know, I know. I'll be there.

Jake: Good.

Me: Hey, I've got news. I ordered a pizza on the phone and went to pick it up in person.

Jake: Yes! I knew your girl would motivate you.

Me: Not my girl, but yeah.

Jake: Proud of you. And hey, this feels like the perfect time to tell you I found someone I want you to talk to.

Me: What, a therapist?

Jake: Sort of. He's a speech therapist who specializes in stuttering because, wait for it, HE has a stutter.

Me: Really?

Jake: Yeah. And here he is with a full career where he talks to people for a living. That proves it's possible bro. You can do it, too.

Me: Huh.

Jake: Listen, promise me you'll at least talk to him once and feel this out. It can't hurt.

Me: Yeah, okay.

Jake: Remember, you're doing what you need to do to claim the life you want and the relationship you want. Pizza was a great start, but you need more.

Me: Yeah yeah, you're right. I know.

Jake: Good, I'll text his name and number over. I already talked to him about you. He's expecting you to reach out, and the number I'm sending is his personal cell.

Me: Wow, okay. Thanks.

Jake: Oh, and Max? Skipping the gym and shoving your face full of late-night pizza isn't behavior recommended by your trainer or your hot girl.

Me: What? I didn't get that last text. I think my phone's dyi...

Jake: Funny. See you.

I watched the phone, waiting for the contact information for the speech therapist to arrive. When it did, I stared at the name in contemplation. Wyatt Levine. His *name* even seemed interesting and sort of magical to me. How had he done it? How had he overcome a stutter and turned a negative experience into a way to help others? The concept fascinated me because, basically, my life had taken the opposite route. I wanted to know his secret, and I desperately wanted to be able to do it, too. Overcome my stutter? Even *conquer* it? It sounded so fantastical to me, like I might as well be considering a fight with a dragon. But, hey, if Wyatt Levine could do it, so could I, right?

I considered typing a message to him then and there, but a burst of bravery and pizza-fueled confidence had me hesitating. Texts are for hiding. I was trying to *stop* hiding, right? What would Wyatt Levine do? He probably wouldn't text. He'd call.

As I decided to do just that in the morning and actually *talk* to him, a vision of Lily's precious face floated into my mind—just as she'd looked at the elevator: breathless and beautiful. The image brought a smile, and it bolstered my confidence even more than the pizza outing had.

I was on the right path, and that journey was leading me toward Lily.

I could do this.

Chapter 26

The Path to Freedom

I DIDN'T THINK about it. I didn't second-guess myself or let my dad's voice have the chance to start screaming in my head. I just did it.

The next morning, after I got home from the gym, I called Wyatt Levine. When he picked up and answered the phone—confidently and with zero hesitations—I could feel a sense of absolute certainty click into place inside me. I was doing the right thing.

"Hello?"

"H-h-hi. This is M-Max Cruz. M-m-my brother J-J-J-...." I was so nervous suddenly that I couldn't even say Jake's name. But the craziest thing was happening, I quickly realized—he wasn't jumping in to finish my words. I mean, come on, if Jake had really talked to him about me, then Wyatt Levine knew precisely who I was and likely what I was trying to say. But he wasn't rushing me or finishing off my opening words. He just...listened. I liked him already, and he'd only said one word to me so far.

I took a deep breath and tried again.

"J-Jake. He said you c-c-could help m-me."

"I'm so glad you c-called, Max," he said. I could hear the slightest trace of his own stutter in his voice, and it comforted me somehow. "What exactly are you hoping to achieve? What are your goals in c-calling me?"

The question dropped into my mind like a rock

hitting still water, and I could feel the rippling effect expanding through my brain and into my soul. What *did* I want?

Well, I wanted to be with Lily, of course. But I also wanted to be a man she could be *proud* to be with. Someone kind, dependable, real, and courageous. Someone with nothing holding him back.

"I w-want to be f-free," I admitted to him, astonished at how quickly and easily I was opening up to a stranger. "I w-want to h-have a real l-l-life."

"Max, you know that there's no c-cure, right?" he said, his voice soft and patient. "It's all hard work and practice, but it's also attitude. You c-can't hide from your stutter or try to bottle it up inside of you. The path to the freedom you described involves owning it. Being proud of this part of you. Just letting it out."

"Wh-what do you m-m-mean?" I asked, astonished by what I thought he was saying. Be *proud* of my stutter? Embrace the very thing that was keeping me locked away from the rest of humanity? Was he nuts?

"Okay, look at it this way," he went on, "have you ever noticed that the more frustrated you get with yourself, and the more you actively try *not* to stutter, the worse it becomes? That fighting it has the opposite effect, and the stuttering gets worse and worse the harder you b-battle it?"

"Yes," I said, my head nodding before I even replied, as if he could see me through the phone. Which actually made some sense, since it felt in that moment like he could see *inside* me. "It's t-t-true."

"And when you're more relaxed," he continued, "and talking with people you know and trust, do the words come more easily? Are you able to c-communicate more freely?"

"I only t-talk to J-Jake," I admitted. "It's easy w-with him."

"Right," he said. "You're simply being yourself with him. You trust him, and that trust opens the doors of c-communication for you."

"Th-that makes s-sense," I said. "B-but how does th-that help me with the rest of the w-world? I c-can't relax and t-trust everyone."

"No, you're right, you can't," he agreed easily. "And there are people out there who will be cruel. That's the brutal truth. But it's not the rest of the world you need to trust, Max, it's *you*. You need to work on relaxing, finding your c-confidence, and yes, embracing this part of yourself. I can help you, but you have to want that help. You have to be willing to love yourself enough to do the hard work, and that means learning to love every part of you, even the stutter. That's where your freedom lies."

"I c-can't even imagine th-that," I said, reeling from his words. "M-m-my d-dad spent a l-lot of years p-p-programming me. I h-hate my s-stutter."

"Jake mentioned your father and how you grew up. And, of course, I'm simply a speech therapist, not a counselor. I'm only drawing on my own personal experience, along with those of my clients over the years. But based on those things, I can tell you with absolute confidence that your dad was *wrong*. He absolutely got it wrong, Max. I don't know if it came from a place of fear or hate or bias, but he filled your head with bad information. Stop listening to what he had to say on this topic, because it's clear from the little bit of information that Jake gave me that his message set you on the wrong path. Would you agree with that assessment?"

"Y-yes," I told him, and I meant it. Obviously, my father's approach had proved to be devastating. And as a result, I'd been trapped inside a bubble. My world was essentially a snow globe, only it was pieces of self-confidence that kept fluttering around me when shaken.

"Max, I don't know exactly what your goals or dreams are for your future, but I can tell you that I'm happily married. I have two kids, and I coach soccer for their teams. I'm active in our community. You already know I have a job I love. My life may not be what *you're* looking for, but it's a full life, and it makes me feel c-complete, happy, and satisfied. Do you feel those things about your current life?"

"N-no," I said immediately. Now his words filled me with excitement at the possibilities about my own future, which was something I never let myself think about much. Lily's face was flashing through my mind again....

"Then think about it," he said. "I'm happy to start meeting with you and working with you. But, like I said, really think it over. It's not going to work if you're fighting yourself."

Again, Lily's face flashed through my mind just as she'd looked at the elevator. I could suddenly see a different ending to that encounter, one in which I reached out and took her hand, pulling her into my arms instead of standing there petrified as the doors closed between us. The image was both beautiful and painful, and I clenched my free hand into a fist of frustration. Wyatt Levine, meanwhile, was outlining a path to freedom, and the only obstacle in it was me. I needed to see this through. I *had* to.

And, if turning that vision into reality meant learning to love my stutter, then, well...I guess my response to that had to be *bring it on.*

"L-let's set up the f-first appointment," I told him.

When I disconnected the call a few minutes later, I was smiling.

Chapter 27

Two Crushes

LIFE IS WEIRD. A couple weeks ago, I was thoroughly wrapped up in my Chad fantasies. They'd always felt so important and such a huge part of my life. After all, I'd been harboring them since childhood. But when Claire told me what he'd said, she essentially stuck a needle in the balloon that held those feelings. When the balloon popped, the feelings and the carefully cultivated library of memories within started to drift upward into cookie-dough-flavored clouds.

It was mind-blowing that, as monumental as all of that had felt in my own life, it hadn't even registered on the opposite side—for Chad himself. I had never even been a blip on his radar, so he never knew I had a crush on him. And I'm sure Claire never told him that she blurted out his true feelings to me. It was as if that crush had never existed at all. My memories of it already felt distorted and distant, like a faint echo from the past.

But none of that was even the weird part. As monumentally life changing as all of that had seemed to me, it was nothing compared to how I felt about Soulful Guy. After only two intense encounters—with, let's face it, a stranger in my building whose name I didn't even know—I was utterly enthralled. There was a magnetic pull yanking me toward him, and it compelled me in a way that nothing about Chad ever had.

Still, though, I haven't gotten to the weird part.

The truly weird part is that while I was busy dissolving longtime feelings about Chad and igniting a burning yearning for a stranger, my thoughts and emotions also seemed to be centering themselves around Cruz. *He* was the one toward whom I found my thoughts mostly wandering. I wanted to share funny comments about my day with him, and not just during our evening chats. Normally that space in my life was solely held by Claire. But lately, when I picked up my phone, it was Cruz's name I was beginning to hunt for first. My story updates, small confidences about my writing dreams, and passing thoughts about the random things that happened in the course of a typical day...I wanted to give all of them to Cruz. Even though I'd never seen him or spoken with him outside of a text, he was quickly becoming a close confidante and friend.

That kind of made me want to ask his opinion about Soulful Guy, but was that weird to talk about one guy with another? Were my feelings for Cruz only about friendship? Had I managed to replace my Chad crush with not one but *two* new crushes?

That thought had me dropping my plastic fork into the to-go salad bowl I was currently digging through in the employees' room at work.

Wait...what? Did I really have feelings for both Soulful Guy *and* Cruz? That wasn't possible, right? I'd always been such a romantic, and I love my romance tropes. But I despise love triangles. I was pretty sure I physically couldn't be living inside of one...*right?!*

But...oh no. This was an emergency, and I needed a woman's opinion, I decided, as I pulled out my phone and shot a text to Claire.

Me: Got plans after work?
Claire: I told my mom I'd stop by tonight, but a

detour to get drinks with my girl should work.

Me: Perfect!

Claire: I probably know what you're going to say, but you wanna come with me to see my mom? She's always asking about you.

Me: And possibly run into Chad?

Claire: Probably not.

Me: But the possibility exists?

Claire: I mean…he's her kid, too, so…

Me: Too soon.

Claire: Okay, I got you. Usual time and place?

Me: Yup.

I felt calmer just knowing I'd be seeing Claire, who could help me sort out my multiple-crush issues over stress relievers like wine or piña coladas. Y'know, like civilized people do.

The afternoon was a mad crush of regular appointments interspersed with dental emergencies, so before I knew it, I was stirring a straw absentmindedly through my drink. And Claire was her usual combination of comfort wrapped in icy slaps of honesty.

"Girl, are you serious?!" she was saying, although her tone was somewhat softened by the fact that she paused to lick some salt off the rim of her margarita. "You have a crush on Soulful Guy *and* Cruz?!"

"I don't know!" I moaned, still stirring the piña colada I'd gone with. "That's why I wanted your opinion on it. I mean, come on, it's so soon after the pixie-Tinkerbell-unicorn incident, right? *Too* soon, really. That's what makes me think none of this is real and that my crazy imagination is running away with me, right?"

"We need a name for that," she said, still obsessing

over her salt. "Unibell? Unipixie? Tinkercorn? Pixicorn?"

"Pixicorn, definitely," I said with a small laugh. "But focus! Pixicorn is the reason that my Soulful Guy infatuation, and maybe my feelings for Cruz, are totally in my imagination, right?"

"Well....," she said, sitting back now and focusing an assessing gaze on me. "I do wonder about the Cruz thing. You don't even know what this guy looks like. Actually, you don't even really know if he even *is* a guy. It could be a teenage girl, seriously. Or an eighty-year-old inmate. All you have to go on is Jake's word, and he's just a hot rando we met in the lobby one day."

"A catfish?!" I hadn't thought about it before, but she had a point. My mind flickered through the things Cruz and I had talked about. Would a catfish make up social anxieties? A rough childhood that somehow involved a bad relationship with his dad? That seemed like a weird way to reel me in, but I guess she was right that the possibility existed.

"I can see your mind churning away over there," she said. "Are you coming up with any reasons to think it might be a scam?"

"I don't know," I said. "I guess it could be, but he's admitted to social anxiety and a toxic relationship with his dad. He's a web designer who lives in California. Those seem like weirdly specific and benign details if he's laying a mantrap that's supposed to get my hormones so stirred up that I'll start wiring money around the world, or whatever the scheme is."

"Yeah," she said, "you're right that it doesn't exactly scream 'catfish.' But keep it in mind anyway. You don't know this guy at all, really."

"And Soulful Guy?" I asked.

"That, my friend, is a different story," she said, smiling at me now. "Lils, I've never seen you like that before. Your energy with him was crazy hot. And at least he lives around here. You could ask him out next time you run into him and see where things go."

"Yeah, I'd love to get to know him," I said, picturing his face when I'd seen him in the elevator, the heat emanating from those brown eyes. "Or even hear him speak. He's never said a word to me."

"Very mysterious," she said. "But, honestly, I'm glad you've got these new crushes to obsess over and to help you get past Pixicorn. I didn't like seeing my girl so devastated."

"Thanks," I sighed. "I just wish it was only one crush. You know how I hate love triangles."

"Enjoy the ride," she said with a laugh. "Just get to know them both. And keep up with your writing. Be your normal, positive self. You've got this."

I realized later, after Claire drove away, that I hadn't actually been successful in getting any answers to my crush questions. As always, she'd made me feel better, sure. But I still didn't know if it was possible for me to have switched off my Chad emotions and switched on feelings for not just one new person but two so quickly. Questions and doubts pummeled me as my mind sorted through my memories of Soulful Guy and my interactions with Cruz. I just didn't know how to process any of it and soon became lost in a fog.

I was so wrapped in my thoughts, in fact, that I didn't even realize there was anyone else near me on the sidewalk…until I saw the knife.

Chapter 28

Saved

"THE PURSE," the man holding the knife growled, his face partially obscured by a hoodie. "Hand it over."

"I…what?" I said, terror and confusion making my thoughts so murky I couldn't process what was happening. Who was this guy? Where had he come from?

"Your purse!" he said again, flashing the knife as he started to reach toward me. "Just hand it over, and you won't get hurt."

I flinched and instinctively took one step back from him and closer to the familiar façade behind me, my mind now noting that I was almost to my apartment building. I was being mugged practically on my own doorstep. And I'd likely sustain serious injury if I didn't snap out of my fuzzy daydreams and do as I was being told.

"H-here," I said, slowly reaching for my crossbody bag. I was going to have to lift it over my head, which felt like an almost inhuman and extremely complicated feat in that moment. My brain was still caught in a web of confusion, and I couldn't seem to process how to accomplish it, making my movements jerky.

"Would you come on?" he said, his eyes shifting around as I drew the bag over myself, my long hair tangling in the buckle on the strap. His patience with my slow movements snapped, and suddenly he was lunging toward me.

I couldn't keep the scream from erupting out of my mouth as he grabbed the purse along with a handful of my hair, yanking both with a violent tug that threw off my balance. I crumpled to the sidewalk awkwardly, dragging my purse down with me.

"Freaking klutz," the mugger muttered, reaching over to grab the purse where my downward momentum had placed it. He hesitated then, like he was mulling over what to do with me, when suddenly a male voice I didn't recognize yelled my name, a sound that seemed tinged with terror. The mugger looked over his shoulder, turned back to me for a second, and then he took off running with my purse still clutched in one hand and the knife in the other.

I stood up slowly, my hands stinging where the concrete had scraped them. Then suddenly I realized someone else was approaching—it was Soulful Guy! A small gasp escaped my lips as I watched him draw closer to me than we'd ever been before. It was like I had wished him into existence, and despite my lingering fear, the moment suddenly felt magical and important. I watched the rise and fall of his chest for a moment and listened to the quietly comforting sound of his slightly ragged breathing. *He ran to me,* I realized.

I drew in a jagged breath of my own as our eyes met. His face looked creased with worry. He opened his mouth to speak, but the words never came. Instead, he brought up one hand and brushed his thumb gently on my cheek. Tears started to gather in my eyes, and he winced at the sight of them.

I was about to do something crazy like walk right into his arms when, with one last worried look, he suddenly took off running in the same direction as the mugger.

"No!" I yelled. "What are you doing? He has a knife!" But Soulful Guy apparently ran track events in his spare time, because he was soon gone from my sight. I wasn't even sure if he'd heard my warnings. I felt stunned and worried, even as part of me distantly wondered if he'd even really been there at all.

I stood there for a long moment, shock and indecision bolting my feet in place, as the events of the last couple minutes replayed in my mind. I'd been mugged. *Mugged!* And at knifepoint! My mom would have a freaking cow if she knew. They'd probably have to sedate her.

I didn't know what to do. Should I call the police? My phone and keys were in my pocket, so I technically could call. But I hadn't really gotten a good look at the guy and probably couldn't give them much of a description. I'd been so shocked and slow to react that I hadn't even thought about looking him over for identifiable scars or tattoos or whatever. I wasn't even sure what color hoodie he'd been wearing.

I wished Soulful Guy would come back. I'd felt so soothed and safe in his presence, and I wanted nothing more than to get another chance to walk into those arms. Our encounter floated through my mind again; I could still feel his gentle touch on my cheek.

As my indecision stretched out, I realized that as much as I wanted to wait for Soulful Guy, I also just wanted to go home. I was scared and upset and still hurting from the fall I'd taken. I waited a few minutes more, then willed myself to start walking, my steps taking me closer to the apartment and farther from where I'd last seen him. I went into the building, pausing to search the sidewalk one last time for him, still wishing with everything inside me that he'd come back. But there was no sign of him. In the end, I trudged over to the elevator and finally made my way home.

Once I was safely locked inside, I went to the bathroom and got undressed, assessing my injuries. The scrapes on my hands weren't terribly deep and would heal quickly. There was a tender spot on my hip where I'd landed. It might produce a bruise in a day or two. My scalp was sore where he'd grabbed my hair trying to get my bag, but I didn't think he pulled any out.

All told, I'd gotten pretty lucky. I hadn't been carrying any cash, although I guessed that I would need to contact the bank and cancel my debit card. When I remembered that my driver's license was in my wallet, I had a brief moment of panic. The thought of having to go to the DMV and deal with the lines and the forms was probably the worst part of any of it. Then my imagination really got going once I thought about what could happen if the mugger used the information to steal my identity or start setting up fake accounts in my name. Or if he used it to come to my apartment to find me...I took a deep breath and tried to tamp back the panic attack that was working to overtake me.

I'm safe, I'm alive, and I'm essentially uninjured.

That's what mattered most, I reminded myself as I stepped into the shower and tried to wash away the memory of the fear I felt when he lunged at me. He lunged, I screamed. *And....*

I turned the shower off as the next memory came back to me. Someone had called my name! The mugger had heard the sound, stopped focusing on me, and took off. Someone had called my name, and then the next thing I knew, Soulful Guy was standing there, looking like he'd run to reach me. My eyes flew open as the picture came into focus in my mind. Soulful Guy knew my name because he'd been there the day I met Jake. Soulful Guy called out my name and, in doing so, might have saved my life! Wow, sure, okay...but why had he run off? Was he really chasing the mugger down? That's what I thought initially, but....

I toweled off, pulled on my coziest sweats, and zipped myself into a warm, fleece-lined hoodie. I just wanted to feel snug and safe and secure while I went about canceling my cards and figuring out how to replace everything.

But as I padded out of the bedroom, I heard a knock at my door. My heart jumped in fear for a moment. The mugger had my address in my purse. Maybe he'd come to finish what he'd started. But wait...do murderous thieves knock politely? That thought had me inching toward the door, where I looked out the peephole. The hallway appeared empty, so I cautiously opened the door and then gasped at what I saw.

My purse was hanging on the doorknob.

Chapter 29

Not a Rock Star

I GRABBED MY PURSE off the doorknob and looked wildly down the hall in the hopes of spotting Soulful Guy, but there was no trace of him.

I pulled the door shut again and locked it once more, then I unzipped my purse. My wallet was still inside. So that meant I still had my debit card, driver's license, the little fortune I'd saved from a cookie at my favorite Chinese restaurant, the picture of Marshmallow, the cat I'd had when I was growing up—all of it. Everything was there.

I couldn't believe it. He'd saved me! Soulful Guy had scared off the mugger, then he chased him down, retrieved my purse, and returned it to me. I'd been way off base. Soulful Guy wasn't a rock star. He was a *superhero*.

I collapsed onto my couch, still holding the purse in amazement. But I also found myself wondering about something—why didn't he stay and let me thank him? Or at least find out what had happened?

I closed my eyes and let the events of the evening scroll through my mind. First, my confusion and terror. Then my fall to the sidewalk, and the sound of my name ripping its way out of Soulful Guy's mouth. There was no other way to describe it. He'd seen me in danger, and he'd run straight into that same danger without hesitation.

Then there was the way he'd *looked* at me, and the

gentle thumb caressing my cheek! It *had* to be proof that I affected him the way he affected *me,* right? Okay, so why had he never spoken to me? And why wasn't he here with me *right now?*

I leaned my head back and stared sightlessly at the ceiling, the events of the evening continuing to loop through my thoughts. I needed to talk to someone. As much as I wished it was Soulful Guy himself—who already knew precisely what I'd been through—I had no way to contact him. And he apparently didn't want to talk to me or check on me anyway.

There was no way I could tell my parents about this, either. I wasn't exaggerating about my mom before. Her worrying was already at Mount Everest elevations. If I told her about any of what happened, she'd have me mounted inside a glass box for my protection.

I thought about texting Claire, but she was at her mom's, so I didn't want to ruin their time together. Plus, I didn't want her feeling guilty for not driving me home. I'd insisted that I was fine walking, so it was my fault regardless.

Cruz....

Yeah, I needed to talk to Cruz.

*   *   *

I pulled my phone out of my hoodie pocket; I'd luckily stored it there earlier, so it hadn't been part of the mugging fiasco. I took a minute to look it over and was relieved to see that it didn't seem damaged in any way from my fall to the sidewalk.

Me: Hey, can I talk to you? Is now a good time?

His reply came quickly, which helped to soothe my jangling nerves.

Cruz: Sure. How are you?

Me: Honestly, not great. I got mugged tonight.

Cruz: What??? Are you okay????

Me: Yeah, I'm fine. Well, I've got some scrapes and bruises.

Cruz: Tell me what happened.

Me: Claire and I had gone for drinks after work, and after that I was walking home alone. I was thinking about everything she and I had been talking about, and I was totally distracted. So, basically, I did exactly what everyone tells you not to do. I wasn't aware of my surroundings at all.

Cruz: Lily, listen to me, whatever happened wasn't your fault.

Me: Yeah, I know. I guess. But I seriously wasn't paying attention.

Cruz: Not. Your. Fault.

Me: Lol, okay okay. So I was paying a not-my-fault amount of attention to my surroundings, when suddenly I realized there was someone there. And he had a knife.

Cruz: You must have been so scared.

Me: I was. He kept telling me to hand him my purse, but it was like I couldn't figure out how to do that. My mind froze or something.

Cruz: Then what happened?

Me: I was trying to get it over my head, but my hair got tangled. Then he reached for it, and when he yanked on it, he grabbed some of my hair, too. The purse and I both fell over.

Cruz: That was probably a good thing. It might have kept him off balance or distracted or something.

Me: Maybe. He reached down to get the purse, and then he kind of stopped, like he was thinking about

Cruz: Lily? Are you still there?

Me: Sorry. Crying. Had to get a tissue.

Cruz: I wish I was there to help. I'd be holding out my arms to you right now.

Me: Cruz, if you were here, I'd happily walk right into those arms. I really, really want that hug.

Cruz: You're getting a long-distance hug right now, though. It's helping, isn't it? Admit that you're impressed.

I couldn't help the short laugh that escaped through my sobs. Talking this out with him was exactly the therapy I needed on short notice. But yeah, not going to lie…I *really* wanted that hug.

Me: Stop interrupting my crying with laughter, Cruz. Gah, so selfish.

Cruz: You're killing me here, Lily.

Me: Actually, I haven't even gotten to the crazy part of the story yet. Remember I told you that my book idea was somewhat based on a real experience I'd had recently?

Cruz: Yeah.

Me: My rock star showed up right at that moment. Not only did he scare off the mugger, he chased him down and got my purse for me!

Cruz: Really? Wow.

Me: Yeah, I totally got it wrong, Cruz. He's not a rock star.

Cruz: He's a long-distance runner?

Me: Ha, no. He's a superhero.

*   *   *

I felt so much better after our conversation. He asked me a million times if I was okay, then I pulled up the blanket that lives in a heap on my couch and snuggled under it. I felt exhausted from the events of the day and the long cry I'd just had. I thought about how Soulful Guy had saved me, and about how Cruz had been there for me when I needed him.

I'd gone out for drinks with Claire in hopes of sorting through my feelings for both of these fascinating guys. I didn't have any answers yet, but the events of the evening had crystallized one thing for me at least: My feelings for them weren't a byproduct of the Chad / Pixicorn situation. Yes, I'd met both guys immediately after. But the timing was just a coincidence. I didn't have these feelings because I was compensating for the pain Chad caused me. Actually, Chad had done me a favor. If he hadn't devastated me, I wouldn't have been in my lobby with Claire that day. I wouldn't have seen Soulful Guy. And Jake wouldn't have put me in contact with Cruz.

Just as that thought was lifting the corner of my mouth in a small surge of happiness, I glanced at my purse, then did a doubletake. There was a mark on it that I hadn't noticed before. I picked it up off the floor and looked at it more closely. It was a dark smear on the pink leather. I stared at it for a long moment, then my eyes opened wide.

It was blood!

Chapter 30

The Tackle

SUPERHERO? *Superhero?!*

The word kept repeating in my head as I stood in the shower watching the blood run down the drain. Lily thought of *me*, Max—the guy who couldn't bring himself to say one word to her—as a *superhero*. My mind was absolutely blown.

I wasn't trying to show off for her. It wasn't like I'd been thinking about ways to make myself look good in her eyes. It all just…happened. And fast, too. The entire incident was a blur now, the way the people on the ground look when you're going past them on a carnival ride.

The evening had actually started out pretty great. I'd met with Wyatt Levine—he'd urged me to just call him Wyatt, but he seemed too spectacular in my mind for that. It's kind of like how people use full names when they talk about famous actors or singers. He was standing in that kind of a spotlight in my mind. I'd been enthralled by the mere idea of him when Jake made the recommendation, but now that I'd actually met him? Not gonna lie, I practically *revered* the guy. He was everything I wanted to be, and he was willing to help me get there. Incredible.

We didn't do a whole lot in that first meeting. He just sort of talked to me—about his own struggles and how he overcame them, some of the strategies that had worked for him, and a variety of exercises and techniques his other clients had found useful. It felt like we were old buddies catching up or something, but I think maybe that was the whole point. He probably just wanted me to start feeling comfortable with him. Whatever his reasons, all I know is that it was working, and I felt very at ease. I found myself talking openly with him, something I'd reserved only for Jake over the years. It felt astonishing to so quickly reach that level of rapport with someone, but Wyatt Levine was his own kind of superhero.

When I left, he gave me some strategies to try, along with the website for the Stuttering Foundation. He said I should dig through their materials, watch some videos, and generally familiarize myself with the most current advice. I could do that. No, I was *happy* to do that. No problem. I wanted to do absolutely anything that would bring me closer to becoming a man worthy of Lily. Videos? Strategies? Practice drills? Bring it on.

That was what I was thinking about when I rounded the corner and heard her scream. I'm not sure how or why I knew it was Lily, but I did. It was like my *heart* knew—and yeah, I know that's corny, but I swear it's true. The kind of adrenaline that helps people lift cars and perform other superhuman feats in times of danger, that's what spiked through me. And before I could even think about it, I was roaring her name and racing toward the man menacing her. I didn't know he had a knife at the time, but that knowledge wouldn't have slowed me. I only knew I had to get to her. Nothing could have stopped me.

When he took off running, I was torn between chasing him down and checking to make sure she was okay. I chose Lily...at least at first. The fear and the unshed tears in her eyes gutted me, though. She was afraid, and now that creep had her purse. I didn't want him to have any piece of her. I wanted those clouds of terror to clear away, allowing her natural sunshine to return. I also wanted to find the guy and take back his power over her, but I couldn't resist touching her first—something I'd never been able to do before. So I ran my thumb down her cheek in a caress that carried with it a lifetime of longing, then ran off like a coward. If I'd stayed another second, I'd have been forced to speak to her, and I just couldn't do that yet. I wasn't ready to see the attraction in her eyes melt into confusion and pity. I just couldn't.

What I *could* do is run. Thanks to Jake's nagging about my gym time, I was a cardio king. I could have chased that mugger all evening if necessary, but clearly he'd been spending his hours committing crimes instead of working out, because I gained on him pretty easily. I don't think he expected the need for a solid getaway plan, because he was practically sauntering only a block or two from where I left Lily. That's when he heard my thudding footsteps, looked over his shoulder, and bolted.

I chased him for several more blocks, but soon he was slowing down and looking around like he was trying to find something—maybe a fence to scale like in the movies or whatever. When I closed the gap, that's when I realized how dumb I was being. He turned around and swiped a knife in my direction, but it was too late. I had launched myself and was already midair, going in for a lower-body tackle. I grabbed at the purse as we both hit the sidewalk, an audible *Oof!* bursting out of him as we landed. I held onto his legs with one arm; Lily's purse was still tightly clenched in my other fist.

Since I had no plans of letting go, I wasn't exactly free to start punching him. I'd never been in a fight before, though, and I confess I wasn't really sure what I was supposed to do next. In the end I just held on fiercely while he struggled to get back on his feet.

"I don't need this," he muttered, kicking me repeatedly while thrashing around until he finally worked out of my grasp and scrambled away. I watched for a stunned moment as he ran off again, not sparing another glance back.

I stood up in a daze as I gradually realized two things—I still had Lily's purse in my hand, and blood was oozing down my arm. He'd sliced me fairly deep in my left forearm when I tackled him. I wasn't even sure he realized this since it all happened so quickly. I looked around for the knife, but I didn't see it anywhere. He must have hung onto it during the fall.

I walked home in a daze, my arm throbbing while one terrifying thought burrowed deep in my mind— *What if Lily had been the one injured?* A vision of me finding her crumpled on the sidewalk instead of the way it actually unfolded had me almost doubled over in pain. I stopped a minute and worked to slow my breathing. *That wasn't what happened, okay? She wasn't injured. She's safe.* Those thoughts had the desired effect, and soon I was breathing normally enough to keep moving forward.

I tightened the grasp on my arm, where I was attempting to slow the bleeding long enough to get home. I wondered distantly if Lily would be waiting somewhere, but the lobby was empty as I made my way over to the elevator. When I got to our floor, I hesitated at her door. I desperately wanted to know if she was okay, but I also didn't want to scare her. I looked a little like I'd just wandered off the set of a horror movie. She didn't need to see that, and I wasn't ready to talk to her anyway. With a pang of regret, I hung her purse on her doorknob, unlocked my own door so I could make a fast getaway, then stepped back quickly and knocked on hers. I closed my door after that as silently as possible, then listened for the sound of her opening hers and closing it again. She was home, and she was safe.

Nothing else mattered.

Chapter 31

Stitches and Bonds

OKAY, SO the bleeding wasn't stopping. If I bled to death in my bathroom, that would be a pretty lame ending for a superhero. That thought had a tiny smile tugging at the corner of my mouth as I pulled out my phone.

Me: Do you think urgent cares do stitches?

Jake's reply was almost instantaneous.

Jake: Max wtf?

Me: Duh, I need stitches dude. Try to keep up.

I didn't want to worry him, but I'd never gotten injured like this before. I seriously didn't even know what to do. Go to the urgent care? The emergency room? Call my regular doctor? Get out a needle and thread? I had no idea.

Jake: Not funny. Seriously, what happened?

Me: A knife happened.

Jake: OMG stop joking around. I'm on my way.

Me: Jake come on I'm just kidding. Chill out. It's nothing.

Jake, of course, did not chill out—and, to be fair, it wasn't really nothing. Soon he was knocking at my door. I had a bloody towel tied awkwardly around my arm as I pulled the door open, after which Jake's eyes looked like they were going to pop out.

"Bro, I'm about two seconds from calling an ambulance," he said, his expressions frantic now. "So unless you want your girlfriend to come out into the hall and see you carted off on a stretcher, you better start talking."

"J-Jake s-stop it. I'm okay, r-really," I said, peeling the towel back so he could see. "J-just a scratch, s-see?"

"Maxwell, you're killing me right now," he said, unable to pull his gaze from the gory mess. "Tell me what happened."

So I told him, starting at the beginning of my evening and the Wyatt Levine visit. Then about walking home and hearing Lily scream. How all I could think about when it happened was keeping her safe and making sure that dirtbag didn't get away with her things. And about my flying tackle, the knife, and the lamely weak scuffle that ensued.

"T-turns out I don't know how to f-fight," I said, shrugging my shoulders. "I j-just hung onto his l-legs like a p-piranha."

Jake looked stunned. He didn't respond. He didn't fuss over me or ask questions. He just stared until I started to feel self-conscious and a little ridiculous.

"*What?!*" I asked, defensive now. "He s-scared her. He c-could have h-hurt her. I *had* to do s-something."

"Maxwell," Jake finally said, his voice crackling with emotion. The sadness in his voice really caught me off guard in that moment. "I know you're my brother, and I know I'm not that much older than you. But I've spent so much of my life worrying about you and caring for you and wanting good things for you, that I swear I feel more like your dad than your sibling."

"I w-wish I'd had a d-dad half as awesome as you are," I said, meaning every syllable with a furious intensity. "B-but you know you d-don't really have to w-worry about me. I'm g-going to be okay."

As I said those words, I also realized I fully meant them. And I wasn't just talking about the injury, either. I meant it in *general;* I was starting to believe that I was going to make it and maybe even thrive one day. That kind of confidence was an entirely new sensation for me. I wasn't sure if the source was my meeting with Wyatt Levine, the budding friendship I was building with Lily in our texts, or the growing attraction I could see in her eyes the few times we'd come face-to-face. I guess it was all of those things rolled together. But it was true; I was changing. Growing. Becoming stronger. Becoming my own man in a way I hadn't been able to envision before.

I'd needed Jake and leaned heavily on him for a really long time. And that hadn't been fair to him, I realized as I watched him battle back the worried emotions that seemed to be overwhelming him now. I had to stand on my own two feet for my personal well-being, of course, but I needed to do it for Jake's sake, too. I'd never even thought about it from his perspective before, and my selfishness was painful to face.

"I'm s-sorry, J-Jake," I said. "I've a-asked too much of you all th-these years."

"Shut up," he said before pulling me into a hug. "It was never too much. I love you, and I'd do anything for you. Like, for example, wanting to knock you out for tackling a guy with a knife."

"Gee, thanks," I mumbled into his shoulder, my love for him overwhelming me. "But I'm g-going to get b-blood all over y-you."

Jake pulled back then and gave me a steely look, his hand still on the back of my neck.

"I wasn't kidding. If you ever do something this

dumb and reckless and incredibly brave again, I'll beat you myself," he said, shaking his head, that look of astonishment still on his face. "Your feelings for Lily were supposed to blast you out of your paralysis, not launch your action-hero career. Geez, dude, way to overachieve."

I laughed then, in spite of the pain in my arm and the guilt in my chest.

"I l-love you, t-too."

"C'mon," he said. "Let's go get you stitched up. And you probably need a tetanus shot or something."

"L-let me g-get my wallet," I replied, wandering around to try to figure out where I'd dropped it. Yes, I needed to continue growing and learning to stand on my own two feet. But right at that moment, it felt great to let Jake take over the situation.

I finally found my wallet, and I let him lead the way.

Chapter 32

Growing Feelings

AFTER SPOTTING the blood on my purse, I couldn't stop worrying about Soulful Guy. He'd bravely chased down an armed mugger for me, and he didn't even get a thank you for it. And to make things even worse, he must have gotten stabbed!

Then again, maybe the blood belonged to the mugger. Maybe Soulful Guy really *was* a superhero, fighting the mugger over the knife and then delivering the injured perp to the police. I didn't know, and the mystery was killing me. I was obsessed with finding him so I could make sure he was okay. And yeah—I wanted to see him again. To gaze into the deep brown eyes that had earned him the nickname. To walk into his arms the way I had almost done the evening of the mugging. I wanted all of that...and more.

I searched for him everywhere in the following days. I started doing my laundry every time I accumulated even the smallest pile of dirty clothes. I ate at the pizza place down the block way more than my scale said I should. I checked my mailbox so often I was afraid the building owner would start charging me rent for the lobby, too. But it was like Soulful Guy had vanished. Or had only been a figment of my imagination from the beginning. Actually, if it wasn't for the return of my purse and its accompanying blood stain, I'd wonder if he'd really been there at all on the day I got mugged.

Not knowing what happened was making me crazy, but it did bring with it a surprising benefit—because I was so obsessed with finding him, I wasn't dwelling on the mugging itself. I wasn't sinking into anxiety or depression or fear. Like my crush on Chad and my encounters with Soulful Guy, the mugging seemed to be blurring and fading into a hazy wisp of a memory that almost seemed to belong to someone else. Letting it disappear from my mind like that probably wasn't the best coping method. A therapist would likely tell me I needed to confront such memories, talk about them, analyze how they made me feel, and come up with strategies on how to move forward. But I didn't think that was necessary. I mean, come on, I *had* talked about it! I talked about it with Cruz, and he'd made me cry and laugh and feel like everything would be okay. So maybe those tears I'd shed while texting with him were all the therapy I needed.

And speaking of Cruz, we'd been getting closer and closer. I no longer felt like I should wait to text him in the evening—we'd start in the morning and go all day long. We had inside jokes. We had shows we were both watching and loved to analyze together. He told me about the websites he was working on and the crazy clients he dealt with. I told him about the dentist's office and how much I loved it because of all the people I got to meet. And, of course, we encouraged each other. He was usually the first person I talked to every morning and the last person before I went to sleep. The more I got to know him, the more I wanted to know *about* him. He was funny and kind, supportive and honest. Silly and vulnerable...and very real.

It occurred to me, of course, that I could just ask Cruz about Soulful Guy. I could tell him that I was worried and ask him to please check in with Jake about the situation. Part of me was ready to come right out and do exactly that, but my feelings for both guys held me back. I was moving past having a simple crush on Cruz and was instead charging headlong into real, lasting feelings for him. You don't ask the guy you're falling for to check up on the hot guy you're in deep lust with. No matter how delicately I went about it, that just wouldn't be right.

It also didn't feel right to keep up my obsession over Soulful Guy now that I'd acknowledged I was falling for Cruz. As much as I was stalking and lurking in the hopes of finding Soulful Guy, I was starting to feel guilty about those things, too. Since Cruz and I hadn't talked about our feelings or declared that what we had was either romantic or exclusive, I knew my guilt was misplaced. But knowing that and turning those feelings off were two different things.

As I was mixing and stirring all of these issues around in my head, an incoming text chimed. I reached for the phone hoping it was Cruz, and I wasn't disappointed.

Cruz: Hey, how's your day?

Me: If obsessing and analyzing were Olympic sports, I'd be listening to my country's anthem right now.

Cruz: Lol. Everything okay?

Me: Yeah. Just a lot on my mind. I worry about things I can't control.

Cruz: I worry about those things, too. Also about things I could control but don't. Underachiever. Get on my level. (;

Me: Ha, yeah—I do that too, sadly. Hey, so speaking about things we can change, what's today's

challenge for getting out of your apartment and interacting with the world? Another coffee run? Have you leveled up to food shopping yet?

Cruz: I should. The only thing edible here is condiment packets, and some of those might have come with the apartment.

Me: Gross, Cruz. Repeat after me: Grocery run! Grocery run!

Cruz: Lol, yeah, it's next. But not today. I have dinner plans, actually. Placing my order will have to be today's challenge.

A sloshing whirlpool of jealousy hit me so hard that I was momentarily stunned. Cruz, a self-admitted hermit, was going out to dinner? Was it a *date?!* Here I was feeling guilty about lusting after Soulful Guy, and meanwhile Cruz was busy planning romantic dinners? Irritation worked its way into my jealousy, creating a burning feeling in my stomach. *Great, now I'm getting an ulcer,* I thought as I debated how to respond to him. Eventually I decided to go with the direct route.

Me: Cruz, do you have a date? You didn't mention that you were seeing anyone.

Cruz: Me?! No, not that kind of dinner. Actually...well, it's my birthday. Jake insisted we should celebrate.

Me: What?!! Happy birthday! Why didn't you tell me? Wait, are you here in Jersey?!

Cruz: Oh, no, sorry. He's here.

I felt like such an immature jerk for getting so jealous, and then for feeling so ridiculously relieved that it wasn't actually a date. But I decided my reactions confirmed my suspicions: My feelings for Cruz were real. And intense, apparently.

Me: Ooh, send me your address! I'll mail you a birthday card.

Cruz: Wow, you don't have to do that.

Me: I want to! Wait, is that weird? Do you not want to give me your address?

So much time passed before his reply came that I decided that yes, I'd just made things weird. And then I started wondering if I'd just gotten proof that Cruz didn't return my feelings or think of me that way. Was this another Pixicorn situation? Or did he only think of me as a friend? My reign over the lands and people of the friendzone would continue, unchallenged, apparently. I had just decided to go find the cookie dough when his reply arrived.

Cruz: Sorry, got distracted. Jake's here. But sure, I'd love to get a card from you. I'd treasure it, actually.

He followed that response with a second text, this one containing the address of an apartment in a town called Glendale. That information had me searching the internet to find out more about the town, but mostly I just learned it was near Los Angeles. I even looked up the street view photo of the apartment building so I could better envision his world. I tried to picture Cruz living in the sunny weather of California, yet spending his days hiding in the building I was examining. The vision made me sad and more determined than ever to help him.

Even if I did exist solely in his friendzone, I'd never abandon Cruz.

Chapter 33

Lies and Love

I WAS FREAKING OUT and mad at myself for all the lies I'd told Lily, which were stacking up like firewood all around me. If I hadn't started the ball rolling with that stupid lie about California, I wouldn't have needed to drag Mitch into it. But there I was, dragging him in.

When Lily asked me for my address, I shot off a frantic text to him, but it took several minutes for his reply to arrive while my worries and anxiety mounted. I didn't want Lily to wonder why I couldn't instantly produce my own address. What kind of weirdo doesn't know his own address off the top of his head? When Mitch's reply finally came, I was ridiculously relieved that he was answering, but of course then I had to endure big-brother-fueled teasing as well.

Mitch: Email?

Me: No, like actual mail.

Mitch: You sending me a present for your own birthday? Not how it typically works, bro, but I like it.

Me: Lol, no, just shut up and send it.

Mitch: So aggressive. Now I feel like messing with you about it. What's in it for me?

Me: OMG just send it. And when you receive an envelope from someone named Lily, can you just not open it and mail it to me?

Mitch: Sounds suspicious. Everything okay little brother?

Me: Yeah.

Mitch: Being real here. You sure?

Me: Very. But thanks.

Mitch: Since it's your birthday, I'll stop hassling you. Have a great day, Maxwell.

Me: Thanks, Mitch.

When the address arrived, I carefully retyped it for Lily. I was feeling a little better, like I'd managed to avert a major catastrophe. But then—fate being as cruel as it was—I had to keep stacking up my lies on the pile when she responded.

Lily: Wait, what's your last name?

I rolled my eyes in frustration. *Exactly what I wanted to avoid.* I decided to stick as close to the truth as possible, if only to increase the chances that the post office would actually deliver the card. I gave her Mitch's name.

Me: Mitchell. What's yours?

Lily: Evans.

Me: Middle name?

Lily: Lily Beth Evans.

Me: That fits you. I like it.

Lily: What's your full name?

I caught myself typing out my actual name, but I realized what I was doing and quickly changed it to Cruz Mitchell. At least I didn't have to lie about the middle name; I didn't have one. My birth certificate just said Max Cruz. Jake and Mitch had always called me Maxwell, and sometimes even Maximillian or Maximus. But my parents hadn't bothered to put that much energy into naming me. Honestly, they hadn't put much energy into me at all, aside from my mom's desperate attempts to squash my stutter in its early days. Meanwhile, my brothers, who were named after my father, Mitchell Jacob Cruz, both had middle names. The whole thing was embarrassing, really. The entire subject made me feel like an afterthought.

Lily: No middle name?

Me: Nope. Not sure why, but no.

There was a knock at the door; Jake had arrived. I hadn't been lying to Lily about my birthday. It really was that day, Jake really did want to drag me out to a local sports bar to celebrate, and I really was going to try to order my food in person.

Me: Hey, I've gotta go pay attention to Jake now.

Lily: No worries. Have a wonderful birthday! I wish I could celebrate it with you.

Me: Same here!

Her last comment had me reeling as I opened the door.

"H-hang on," I said as Jake walked in. "J-just wrapping this up."

"Talking to your girlfriend?" he asked, a self-satisfied smirk on his face.

"No. T-talking to y-yours," I replied on my way back to my room to grab another minute of peace. I could hear him chuckle at my attempted burn.

What would celebrating my birthday with Lily actually feel like? I wondered. As friends, that celebration would be incredibly fun. Just knowing she existed made me happy, so spending an evening with her would probably be nothing short of amazing. But to celebrate my birthday with her as my *date?* That would be the best present ever.

I started tapping out my next comment.

Me: Seriously, spending my birthday with you would be the best present I could ever receive. You know my world is pretty isolated, so that doesn't

sound like very high praise. But Lily, the truth is that you're everything to me.

I stopped typing. Was I seriously in the middle of declaring my feelings for her? Was I nuts? I couldn't just blab out how much I cared about her in some random text.

But, truthfully, who was I kidding? I didn't just care about Lily. I *loved* her. I loved everything about her. I loved her smile and her sunshiny personality. I loved how easily she could talk to people. I loved her sense of humor and her optimism. I loved how looking in her eyes made me feel like I'd found my home.

But I couldn't say all of that, right? Certainly not on a whim as I got ready to walk out the door with my brother. So, in the end, I chickened out and edited my response—

Me: Spending my birthday with you would be the best present I could ever receive. You know my world is pretty isolated, so that doesn't sound like very high praise. But trust me, it is. Have a great evening!

I grimaced at the bland sentiment and sent it. Then I told myself I'd done the right thing. Anything more would have been an emotional risk I just wasn't ready to take yet.

As I walked back to the living room to talk to Jake, I wondered if I'd ever be ready.

Chapter 34

Dear Cruz

DEAR CRUZ....

I stared at the words I'd written inside the birthday card that I bought on my lunch break, uncertain of what I wanted to say next. Should I keep it light and breezy? Just send a generic birthday greeting and leave it at that? Or should I be brave and say more? Should I tell him that I'm falling for him? That his texts were becoming the highlight of my days, and that while we were busy laughing and joking and making small confidences in each other, it felt to me like we were laying the foundation for a real future together? Would that be an insane risk to take? Maybe. What if I met him and wasn't attracted to him in person? What if he was old or smelled or didn't bathe or any number of unappealing things? Was I being shallow by letting those worries hold me back? Was I being stupid if I didn't?

My mind spun crazily until I wasn't even sure if I should send a card at all.

I quickly shot off a text to Claire, begging her to meet me for drinks; once again, I needed her advice. By the time the office had closed, and I joined her at our favorite meeting spot, I was in the middle of a full-blown meltdown. I summarized my frantic internal debate, then braced myself for her response, which was certain to be brutally frank.

"So, you're thinking about starting a relationship

with a guy you've never seen or spoken to before," Claire recounted as a look that could only be described as horror crawled across her face. "And in doing so, you want to close the door forever on potentially exploring something with that cute guy who literally lives in your building and whose mere presence makes fireworks start igniting inside of you? Do I have that all straight?"

"Yes?" I said with a pained wince, the meek reply coming out like a question.

"Riiiight," she said. "Then I guess you won't mind if I try to track down the mystery guy in your building and go out with him?"

I narrowed my eyes at her. She met my menacing look with a mischievous smile and a sharp laugh.

"That's what I thought," she said. "You still have feelings for both guys, so I don't know why you're so fired up to start or end anything with either of them."

"What am I supposed to do, then?" I asked. "I can't even find Soulful Guy. That's part of the problem. I'm supposed to put my dating life on ice forever, waiting around and tapping my foot on the off chance that he'll magically reappear?"

"Maybe," she said. "Or you could just try to meet Cruz. Don't declare your undying love for him, but you could meet him in person and see if he's who he seems to be. Find out if you have chemistry when you're actually in the same room and not merely on the same continent."

"Yeah…I guess I could do that. He grew up here in Jersey. Maybe he'll come home soon. Or I could even fly out there if that works out better."

"I think that's a better plan," she said, taking a less-than-dainty slurp of her wine. "You've got to meet this guy first. You still don't know for sure he's not a catfish. Speaking of which, if you go out there, be smart. Meet in public, let people know where you are, blah blah safety safety."

"He gave me his address, though," I told her, "so I can mail him a birthday card. If he's a catfish, he's really bad at it."

"Not everyone's a straight-A student, Lils."

"So, what? You're saying he flunked some of his catfish courses but still graduated?"

"Exactly!" she said, looking pleased with herself now.

"You're hilarious. But he's not a catfish. He's real."

"Just find out for sure," she replied, her tone serious now. "The plain truth of the matter is that you don't know this guy. Not really."

"I knew Chad," I reminded her, "and look how that turned out."

"True, but that's just proof that you need to proceed with caution in any relationship. I don't want to see you heartbroken again. I keep telling you this, but it's still true: I need a happy Lily, not a sad one."

"I'm working on it," I assured her, taking a sip of my drink as my mind whirled with ideas of what to do next.

*   *   *

After she dropped me off—there was no way I was going to walk home alone—I eyed the card again. She was right, I decided. I couldn't jump into a relationship with both feet when I still felt so drawn to Soulful Guy. It wasn't fair to anyone.

With that decision made, writing the card suddenly became a much easier task—

Dear Cruz,

Happy birthday! I'm so sorry I'm not there celebrating it with you in person. But when you mentioned that Jake went to see you, it gave me an idea: Why don't we meet and celebrate in person? We've gotten so close recently, and it just feels like the right time to meet face-to-face. When you get this, think about it and let me know if we can launch Project Birthday. Just be forewarned that I'm totally going to collect on that hug you offered me. Come on, you know that long-distance hug was lame. (;

I agonized about how to sign off. I almost wrote *Love, Lily*, but since I'd just gotten done deciding it was too soon to drag my feelings into the friendship, that seemed like a bit much. In the end, then, I just wrote my name and drew a little heart.

I excitedly mailed the card the next day, then started counting and guessing and trying to figure out when he'd get it—and, of course, when I could reasonably expect to hear back from him. Anxious energy coursed through me in the meantime, and I was bubbling with excitement.

I couldn't wait to see what the future held for us.

Chapter 35

Booking a Flight

THREE DAYS trickled by at a pace so torturously slow that a sloth could easily outrun it. Meanwhile, I waited for my card to work its way across the country to Cruz. Three days was much too soon to expect it to arrive, but that's when I started getting excited to hear his response. At five days, it was still easy to assume that it hadn't been delivered yet. But as the second week began, I started worrying that I'd written his address incorrectly. Or forgotten to put a stamp on the envelope. Or that it had been intercepted by terrorists. As my worries multiplied and my guesses and theories got crazier, Cruz said nothing, and his silence stretched out into what felt like eternity.

When two whole weeks had gone by, my excitement withered like a plant I'd forgotten to water. *He had to have received it by now,* I thought. Surely he'd had plenty of opportunity to read it—but in saying nothing, he was saying everything....

He didn't want to meet me.

I had a lot of theories about why that would be the case. Maybe he wasn't confident about his looks. Or in something like his job or some other aspect of his lifestyle. *Or maybe he really is a catfish....* It was also possible he'd given me a fake address...or that I'd pushed every social anxiety button on his personal pain console, setting off alarms and flashing red lights.

Or—and this was the one I thought the most likely—he just wasn't feeling it. I was good enough as a casual buddy to trade kazillions of texts with, but not enough to turn what was mellow and meaningless into something substantial and lasting. My reign over the friendzone would continue. I was the incumbent in its upcoming presidential election, and no one was running against me.

I was starting to feel a little guarded in my replies when he reached out to me with his usual funny texts as though nothing had changed. He'd really been working hard to pretend the whole card situation never happened, and his chipper comments and funny asides were now annoying. He didn't reference the card even once, and his texts weren't any different in tone or content than before. I mean, come on, you'd think he'd at least toss out a comment about having received it and maybe even thank me for the gesture. Or, if he hadn't received it, he'd ask whether I'd sent it. I mean, I know it was just a card and not a big deal. And, of course, I didn't do it for the thanks, but.... I don't know. Something about the whole situation just didn't feel right.

I tried to sink all of that pent-up disappointment into my ongoing hunt for Soulful Guy. Now that Cruz had essentially brushed me off, I definitely wasn't feeling guilty about it anymore. But there was still no trace of Soulful Guy anywhere. I hadn't even caught a glimpse of him since the night of the mugging. I was still worried—what if he had been so seriously injured that he'd been in the hospital this whole time? That thought alone sent a spike of icy dread right through me, until I remembered how he'd returned my purse that night. Anyone with injuries so severe that they'd been bedridden for weeks wouldn't have been able to hang my purse on my doorknob and then knock to get my attention.

As all of these doubts and worries kept up their relentless assault, salvation arrived in the form of an invitation from my parents to visit them in Florida. It was true that I hadn't seen them in a while. It was also true that I hadn't taken any of my annual vacation time yet, and I didn't have any big trips planned that would hinge on me having a stockpile of personal days.

Plus, I just felt like I needed to get away. I was tired of worrying about Soulful Guy, and I was sick of not being able to find him. I was also a little annoyed that he didn't come find *me,* since he clearly knew where I lived. And, finally, I was hurt that Cruz didn't want to meet me. So, all in all, I was feeling a little raw and vulnerable. I'd had three fully fledged crushes in a matter of months, and none of them had yielded even a single date. I didn't want to get sucked into a self-pity quicksand, but those doubts and insecurities were lurking right outside my door. I needed a break and a change of scenery. I wanted…well, honestly, I just wanted my mom.

I asked for an upcoming week off, and as soon as it got approved, I bought a plane ticket. I told Claire where I was going, of course, but I didn't bother mentioning it to Cruz. He was part of what I was trying to get away from, after all.

So I packed a suitcase and left.

Chapter 36

Feeling Brave

I KNOW IT WASN'T Mitch's fault, but he was making me crazy. You'd think he would have mentioned that he was heading out of town for a big photoshoot when I asked him to forward Lily's card to me. But he didn't mention it and he *did* leave, and now I was caught up in my stupid web of California lies. I couldn't tell Lily the real reason why I hadn't received or acknowledged her card yet, and I couldn't come up with any plausible explanation for it that didn't include revealing everything to her. So, I'd been trying to avoid talking about it, but I think it was hurting her feelings. I got the impression she was pulling away from me, which was amping up my stress levels and sending them into the air like a geyser.

I definitely didn't *want* to hurt her, and of course I didn't want to lose her friendship, either. As a result, I had begun to think very seriously about blurting out the truth that I'd been purposely hiding myself from her. Once I did that, though, then I'd need to take the next terrifying step and explain *why*. But I hadn't performed that particular trust-fall into sheer honesty because I'd been harboring these crazy fantasies of waiting until my speech improved. It was hard to let those fantasies go.

But the longer I worked with Wyatt Levine, the more I was beginning to understand and accept the real truth: I wasn't going to find a magical cure. I would always have at least some stutter in my speech. Yes, children often grow out of them, but if you reach adulthood? Well, chances are that you'd lost your opportunity to rid yourself of it permanently.

The really mind-blowing part of all of this was that the longer I worked with him, the more I was becoming okay with the knowledge that I'd stutter for the rest of my life. Yes, of course I was practicing the strategies he suggested in order to find ways to better manage it. But I was also practicing the mindset he was offering to me: The acceptance of my stutter. The *owning* of it. I was able to start making that mental shift because I was beginning to see evidence that he was right. The more I rolled with it rather than fight it, the easier the words came, and I'd begun to tap into a smoother stream of communication. Yes, my progress was barely percep-tible, but I also knew it wasn't merely in my imagin-ation—it was really happening.

So, yes, I could continue waiting for my speech to improve more before opening myself up to Lily. Or I could simply choose to trust her and to believe that she'd walk with me on my journey and be okay with it.

With a burst of courage from all these thoughts building up inside, I sent her a text—

Me: I'm feeling brave today.

Lily: That's great. What are you thinking about tackling?

Me: I'm not sure yet exactly.

Lily: Food shopping in person? That sort of thing?

Me: Bigger, I think.

Lily: Wow.

Me: What about you? Have you ever felt like this? Like you were ready to take on the big issues in your life and just charge at them while screaming?

Lily: Lol, yeah, sort of. Actually...Cruz, did you read my card?

Oh no! I'd never come up with a plausible reason for why I hadn't read it yet. Uh...I wanted to savor the anticipation? I had a paper-cut phobia and didn't want to risk opening the envelope? I'd tossed it aside and forgotten it? Lost it?

Stupid reasons fluttered through my head, and I finally just reached out and chose one, essentially at random.

Me: No! My mail has been messed up lately. The post office isn't delivering it or something. I need to go deal with it, but, well...you know.

Lily: But your social anxieties are stopping you?

Me: Yeah.

Lily: Cruz, I'm so sorry! I've been feeling kind of hurt that you never said anything about it, which was stupid. I should have just asked you. I'm so sorry. I'm a terrible person.

I smacked my head with my open palm in frustration. How had I managed to tangle this around so much that now *she* was feeling guilty? It was time to end this, once and for all. It had gone on too long.

Me: You're the least terrible person I've ever met! Er...texted.

Lily: Thanks. Actually...I feel brave today, too.

Me: Really?

Lily: Yeah, I've been thinking about this guy I have a huge crush on. I think I want to tell him how I feel.

Me: You do?! Wow.

Okay, I know this makes no sense, but hearing Lily talking about her crush on her rock star sent a huge avalanche of jealousy rolling through me. Yes, that's right: I was jealous of the feelings Lily had for...*me!* I know that sounds completely stupid, but it wasn't really *me* she liked, was it? That guy was just her rock star, an elusive weirdo with whom she'd locked eyes a couple of times. He got her purse back, and she called him a superhero. But Lily didn't really know that guy. She knew *me*. Max…well, okay, *Cruz*. Everything seemed off-kilter, and I felt disappointed somehow.

Lily: Yeah, and the more I think about it, the more I want to do it. I'm going to walk right out the door and go see him and tell him how I feel.

Me: Good luck, Lily.

Lily: Thanks! (;

And that was it. She was going to walk out of her apartment and search for her rock star. Which meant it was time for me to reveal myself—and the truth—to her. Let her know the real me and see if she could still have feelings for me once she knew about my stutter.

And once she discovered her rock star and her texting buddy were the same person, what would happen then? How would she react? I had no idea, so I braced myself for the sound of her door opening. This was finally happening. The moment of truth had arrived.

All my questions were about to be answered.

Chapter 37

Knocking on His Door

THROUGHOUT the entire flight and ensuing boring layover, the equally long Uber ride, and even in the relatively brief walk to his apartment door, I was freaking out. Worries from every direction had been pummeling me to the point that I was doubting myself, big time. Was I doing the right thing? Was I about to get the Cruz-version of Chad's unicorns-and-pixies reaction to the idea of dating me?

Or, worse than that, what if this was all a huge deception, maybe related to something truly awful like a sex-trafficking scheme? No one even knew where I was! That thought alone made me stop and shoot a quick text to Claire as her safety warnings scrolled through my head.

Me: I flew to California to meet Cruz. Wish me luck!

As an afterthought, I added his address. At least someone would know where to start searching for my body if this went downhill.

I continued moving forward, but the questions and doubts kept up their relentless assault. Was Cruz even who he said he was? What if he wasn't roughly Jake's age like I'd always assumed? What if this *was* a catfish? What if I knocked on the door and a fifty-year-old investment banker opened it? Or a twelve-year-old girl who'd been pranking me the entire time?

I reached his door and stared at the number, my

body now frozen with fear. What if he had anger issues? What if he smelled bad? What if—

My hand jerked forward as if under its own authority and knocked. I'm not sure how I was able to do that, given how petrified I felt. And yet the echoing sound had summoned footsteps that were now drawing closer.

What if he's a sexist jerk? What if he's mean to animals? What if he's—

The door swung open.

"Jake?!" I heard myself shriek, as relief, confusion, and disbelief warred inside me.

"No, not Jake. I'm his brother."

"Oh. Wait…*Cruz?"* I asked, really confused now.

"What?" he asked, dragging a tattooed hand through his hair, which was longer than Jake's had looked wrapped up in its man-bun. "We're *both* Cruz."

"Huh?!" I said, gaping like a fish now. "I'm sorry, let's back up. Is Cruz Mitchell here?"

The Jake-a-like chuckled and looked a little closer at me before asking, "Wait, are you Lily?"

"Yes," I said, feeling at least a little reassured that he knew my name. "Remember? We met in the lobby of my apartment building."

"We haven't met before," he replied. "My name's Mitch. I have a twin brother named Jake, though. You've clearly met him, but no, you and I are meeting for the first time right now."

"Oh…," I said, trailing off, unsure what I could add to that. *Where was Cruz?* Or, I guess, *who* was Cruz? My earlier doubts seemed validated, and I started to wonder in that moment if someone—Jake, I guess—had been playing a joke on me. "Maybe I should just go."

"Listen, Lily, I know you don't know me, and you

don't have any reason to trust me," Mitch began, "but I think I could clear up our mutual confusion with a simple phone call to Jake. I have my suspicions about what's happening here, but I want to confirm them first before I share my theories with you."

"Oh, um, yeah, okay," I stammered, feeling a little like the butt of a joke with a punchline I still didn't understand.

"You're welcome to come in and use the bathroom or sit on the couch or raid my refrigerator or do whatever would make you feel comfortable, but I know you don't know me," Mitch reiterated, shrugging his shoulders. "I don't want to make you feel weird."

"Oh," I said, biting my bottom lip as I thought about it. I knew it was probably dumb to walk into a random guy's apartment, but curiosity and the desire to find Cruz compelled me to stay and try to find some answers. "I guess I'll just wait on the couch then, if that's okay?"

"Yeah, sure, come on in," he said, standing back to let me go by. I walked directly into the small living room, which was bathed in golden afternoon light. Random thoughts about the astonishing beauty of the view from the large windows floated through my mind as Mitch gestured toward the couch. "Can I get you anything to drink before I make that call?"

I shook my head and went awkwardly to the couch before sinking into it.

"Lily, if this is what I think it is, it's a *good* thing," he said, giving me a sexy half-smile. "I promise."

"Okay," I said. "Thank you for trying to help me figure this out."

He walked down a hall, and I could hear him close a door. I looked around the room then, rampant curiosity and my usual wild imagination fueling a search for anything personal that might give me some clues as to what was happening. A story about insanely hot, tattooed twins started to write itself in my head, but the apartment wasn't exactly filling in the details. Actually, it looked like a pretty bare bachelor pad, with no framed pictures or trinkets to help me figure out what happened or where Cruz was.

Eventually I started getting tired. So much time went by, actually, that I began to drift off. Then I heard his voice again.

"Lily?" he said softly. "I think I have your answers."

Chapter 38

The Long Story

I SNAPPED AWAKE, my eyes wide. "Did you find Cruz?"

"Yeah," he said, "but it's a long story."

I watched as he sat in the deep armchair to my right, and I angled my body toward him so I could take in every detail.

"I'm dying here," I said. "What's going on?"

"Well, I'm not sure where to begin exactly, but I guess I'll start by saying that Jake and I have a brother," he said. "A younger brother."

"Cruz?"

"No, Cruz is our *last* name," he said. "His first name is Max."

"Max?"

"Yeah, Max Cruz. And I think he's who you're looking for. I guess he introduced himself to you as Cruz. Well, I take that back. As I understand it, *Jake* introduced you to our brother Max as this guy Cruz—also the guy you've been texting."

"Oh," I said as I tried to make sense of this. "Does he use his last name as a nickname? Kids in school called him that or something?"

"Nah. Like I said, it's kind of a long story."

"Okay, so...did your brothers play a joke on me?" I could feel tears start to well up in my eyes at the thought of this. Chad called me "Silly Lily," and mere hours later I let myself become the subject of some sort of prank? Yeah—classic.

I dashed the tears from my eyes when I saw Mitch shake his head no.

"No, no way," he said. "That's not where this is heading, I promise. Both of my brothers are awesome guys, I swear."

I studied his earnest expression and saw only honesty reflecting back at me. If he was lying, he was a champion at it.

"Okay, I'm listening," I said with a small sniff. "You have a younger brother named Max, and he's the one I've been corresponding with."

"Yeah," he said. "Max never intended to get in touch with you, and he certainly never wanted to lie to you. Jake greased all those wheels."

"If Jake wasn't somehow pranking me," I said, "then I don't understand why he'd do that."

"What you have to understand is that Max has had a really tough life. *Really* tough."

"Oh...wait. Yeah, I guess I knew that already. Because of your dad, right?" He nodded. "Okay, yes, he told me he had a rough childhood and that's why he moved to California. He said he wanted to be anywhere his dad wasn't."

"All of that was true except for the California part. I'm the one who moved out here to escape our dad. Max moved, too. But not out of state."

"Oh," I said. "Wait, hang on—he lives in *New Jersey?* Why wouldn't he just tell me we lived near each other? Unless he didn't actually like me or want to meet me?"

"I'm getting to that part," he replied. "Stay with me here. Like I said, it's a long story."

"Okay, sorry," I said with an apologetic wince.

"Max's troubles started when he was pretty young,

because that's when he first developed a stutter," Mitch went on. He paused then, his eyes searching mine.

"A stutter?" I asked, if only because he seemed to want me to respond.

"Yeah. It started small, but it got worse pretty quickly." He was watching me very closely now, as though the news of Max's stutter would send me screaming from the room. "The more he stuttered, the nastier our dad became. Dad made fun of him; he belittled him. He'd ask him questions and then cut him off when the answers didn't fall easily out of Max's mouth. It was like he was testing Max, knowing that he'd fail each time. Essentially, he engaged in constant psychological warfare against Max for years."

"Oh no....," I whispered. I was devastated by what he was telling me as I tried to match it up with what I knew about Cruz. "He told me he has social anxiety."

"Yeah, thanks to our dad, he sure does. What should have been something pretty common, something that's routinely dealt with in speech therapy, became this devastating, crippling, torturous burden for Max. Something that his own body was committing against him, if that makes any sense. Rather than master it or at least deal with it, he started sinking deeper and deeper into it because of the stress my dad was constantly stirring up. And the worse it got, the uglier things got with the old man, too. The garbage he said would have ripped apart anyone unlucky enough to hear it, and Max was just a kid."

"So what happened?" I asked, stunned. I just couldn't reconcile the funny, caring guy I'd gotten to know with the person Mitch was describing. My heart ached, and I could feel the tears starting to blur my vision again.

"One day the old man snapped," Mitch said, a haunted look in his eyes. "He asked Max a question, and of course Max couldn't respond fast enough for his liking. I don't know why that particular day was different from any other, but my dad drew back his fist. Before any of us could react, he'd knocked him out cold. Max dropped right to the floor."

I gasped and covered my mouth with my hands. Mitch didn't even seem to notice; he just continued speaking.

"Jake and Mom took him to the ER, where he was diagnosed with a mild concussion. Mom told them some fairytale about him getting hit by a baseball."

"What did *you* do?" I asked, a little afraid by the look of pure hatred in his eyes now.

"I...I was very, *very* angry that day. But, well, I don't want to get into all of that. And this is about Max, not me. The thing is, Max doesn't remember any of this anyway, at least consciously. But that was the day it happened."

"The day *what* happened?" I asked, terrified to know the answer and yet somehow unable to stop myself. "He developed social anxiety that day?"

"More than that, actually," Mitch said. "That was the day he stopped talking altogether."

"*What?!*"

"Yeah. He didn't say another word from that day on. Well, that's not quite true. Eventually he did start talking to Jake again. But no one else. And he hasn't for years."

Chapter 39

The Fog Lifts

MAX HASN'T talked to anyone for years?!

Those words rolled wildly in my head as I worked to process their implications.

"That's not true, though!" I said, putting the story together in my mind. "He's been working on it! He was helping me realize my dream of writing a book, and I was helping him overcome his social anxiety. He told me that! He went out and ordered a coffee in person. And he ordered take-out, too! He's done all kinds of things. I've been so proud of him."

"Yeah, I know, and that's exactly what Jake hoped would happen."

"Oh, yeah," I said, thinking back to when I'd first met Jake. "He heard me talking with my friend Claire about how I needed a writing buddy, and he suggested his friend Cruz. But wait, why wouldn't he have just given me Max's real name?"

"Max has spent his life hiding his stutter, so Jake was trying to proceed carefully. He knew Max didn't want to take the chance of running into you and having to speak. Max knew that would be awkward, and he didn't want you to pity him. I'm guessing that's why he told you he lives in California."

"What? I wouldn't have done that!" My mind was whirring now as I tried to match up Mitch's words with what I knew. "Wait…how could I have run into him, though? I wouldn't even know who he was anyway!"

"Lily," he said, a grin on his face now, "Max is your next-door neighbor."

"*What?!*" I asked, feeling both incredulous and, all of a sudden, a little snarky. "Mrs. Henderson?"

"Very funny. No, your *other* neighbor."

"Oh, yeah…I *do* have another neighbor. But I've never even seen them before. He or she…they're so quiet, and they never seem to be home."

"Oh, he's home. Too much. And you've met him. According to Jake, anyway."

"What do you mean?" I asked, even as the clues to the mystery were starting to come together in the fuzzy corners of my mind.

"Jake told me that Max saved you from a mugging."

My mouth dropped open, and in that moment the fog in my mind lifted while the puzzle pieces began snapping into place.

Suddenly I could see Soulful Guy in my mind as he'd looked that day we first saw each other in the lobby. I could still feel the electric pull toward him. Then the vision in my mind leaped forward in time, and I pictured him as he'd looked the day we saw each other at the elevator, and how the heat and fiery longing seemed to radiate from him. Then my thoughts turned to the day he'd interrupted the mugging and touched my cheek for a magical instant before racing off to get my purse.

Cruz is Max. Max is Soulful Guy. And therefore Cruz is Soulful Guy….

It was like a complicated math problem. But it was also suddenly clear and stunningly obvious. I felt like one of those GIFs with incomprehensible symbols, equations, and formulas floating in the air in front of me as I tried to make sense of everything.

"Soulful Guy," I said when I finally pulled my jaw back up off the floor. "That's how I've been referring to him since I didn't know his name."

"Yeah," Mitch said, chuckling now. "That fits. Max *is* soulful. And he's a great kid, not to mention the strongest person I know. He's been doing all those things he told you about to practice social interactions, but he's also been meeting with a speech therapist who Jake set him up with. All very recent changes, and all for the better. It's been a really long time since he stopped talking or trying. He's been frozen since then and locked inside of himself for years. *Years*, Lily. Since the day our sperm donor tried to extinguish his light. But here he is, fighting against the fears, working on his issues, and saving your butt in his free time."

I laughed then, in spite of all the horrible things I'd learned. Mitch was right: Max was amazing.

"How was he able to do it, though?" I asked. "What changed? Where did he find the strength?"

"That's easy," Mitch said. "Look in the mirror."

"Huh?"

"Lily, Max didn't see you for the first time that day you met Jake," Mitch said. "Apparently, he heard you laughing through the walls when you moved in, and he developed a bit of a crush on you."

"Me?!" I said with clear disbelief. "No, no way. I'm the reigning queen of everyone's friendzone. No one's ever had a crush on *me* before."

He chuckled again and looked at me for a thoughtful moment, like he was trying to decide which words to use.

"I don't know about those other guys, who were all super dumb, by the way. I'm just telling you what

Jake told me. Apparently, Max confessed his feelings to Jake, who saw them as Max's ticket out of the prison he'd been locked in for way too long. Jake thought that getting to know you might be the right kind of incentive to make Max finally reach for a different life. When they saw you in the lobby, Jake jumped at the opportunity. He said when the fireworks started sparking off you two, he knew he'd stumbled across a brilliant plan."

"I'm blown away," I said, sniffling now. "I'm not the heroine in anyone's romance. Ask every guy I've ever dated."

"None of what or who came before matters. *Max* thinks you're amazing. I wasn't kidding that he's had feelings for you for a long time. Once he started getting to know you, I guess that was it. The switch flipped. He wants to be worthy of you. He wants to be someone you could be proud to be with and not be ashamed of or embarrassed by."

"But he didn't have to do any of those things," I said. "He was awesome the first time I saw him."

"And that's why I think this is the best thing that's ever happened. Jake's a freaking genius. There aren't many people Jake and I would trust when it comes to Max, you know."

"Okay, so why are you all the way out here?" I asked, awkwardly changing the subject the moment the thought popped into my head. I hoped it wasn't too personal a question. "I mean…if you don't mind me asking. It seems like Max could have benefitted by having both his brothers around."

"I've been thinking about it," he said. "I had a bunch of stuff I needed to work through, but maybe someday."

He looked like he was lost in thought as a quiet settled between us then. My brain was spinning wildly with all I'd learned, the overriding emotion being sheer excitement. I couldn't wait to finally meet Cru…er, Max face-to-face. Simply looking at him lit me up inside. But now? I couldn't even imagine how momentous it would feel to be with him after learning exactly who he was and how we felt about each other.

"Mitch?" I asked, suddenly overwhelmed with the need to see Max as soon as possible. "I have to book the next flight home."

Chapter 40

The Visitor

SHE'D BEEN GONE too long. Something was wrong. Maybe she'd had an accident or something. A vision of Lily lying in a hospital bed somewhere, hurt and alone, flashed through my head, but I shook it off as quickly as it appeared. *No, no, no…please let her be okay,* I silently begged the universe.

I could just text her, right? And she'd probably text right back. Sure…. Then I'd know she was perfectly okay. But I'd also know that it wasn't me she went to find that day. I don't know why I'd ever imagined someone like Lily would declare such feelings to me. I'd never even spoken to her.

No, it wasn't me she had feelings for; it wasn't her silent rock star. She'd told me she was going to go out and find the man she had feelings for and tell him face to face. My face burned with embarrassed heat that I had actually thought she meant me. I had planned to open my door when I heard her leave her apartment and finally reveal to her that we were neighbors. Then, when she saw me, I thought she'd…well, that dream wasn't going to be a reality. Obviously.

For one thing, her door never opened. She never appeared. It was a couple days at that point, and there just wasn't any way to spin it where I'd come out of this with my heart intact. Maybe the unthinkable had happened, and she really was hurt or sick.

My next guess was almost too painful to consider, but, well, my other guess was that it was Chad she meant before. Chad, the jackwagon who'd made her cry. He was probably holding her in his arms that very minute. He'd insulted her and called her names, but if she'd walked right up to him and confessed her feelings, maybe he'd at least have been smart enough to see how beautiful she was and take advantage of the situation. Maybe the whole time I'd been waiting and wondering, they'd been holed up together at his place, talking, laughing, kissing…and living out the future I wanted with her. Maybe all my effort and work to fix myself had simply come too late.

A fiery pain threatened to overwhelm me then, and I tried to purge the realization that it was already too late for Lily and me from my mind....

Then I realized the banging sound I heard wasn't the pain in my head—it was someone at the door. Maybe I'd ordered something and forgotten. Or maybe Jake was making another welfare check. I woodenly walked over and pulled the door open. Normally I check the peephole first, but my mind was in such a tortured state that I didn't even care who it was.

I couldn't contain a shocked inhale when I found Lily standing there. Beautiful, sunny, precious Lily. And she was smiling at me, with the handle to a wheeled suitcase in one hand and a backpack hanging from the other.

My mouth fell open in surprise, and my eyes widened.

"H-h-how....," I stammered before stopping in shock. *What am I doing?!* I'd never spoken to her before, so she didn't know about my stutter! What would she think? I stared for what felt like a long time, confusion and shock rattling my thoughts around in my head like a gambler shaking his dice.

"Hi, Cruz," she said simply. "Or should I call you *Max?*"

I took a deep breath and closed my eyes. When I opened them again, she was still standing there, looking at me with her usual sweet calm sweeping off her in waves. This was *Lily*. I needed to stop freaking out and try to understand what was going on.

"Y-y-you know?" I finally asked, letting my stutter fall right out of my mouth into the space between us. *Wyatt Levine would be proud of me,* I thought as I watched her, waiting to see how she'd react to it for the first time. I didn't see any immediate signs of pity or revulsion. Actually, it sort of looked like she had a teasing glint in her eyes—exactly the same sort of joking manner, I realized, that she always maintained in her texts.

"Oh, I know a *lot* of things, Max," she said coyly, "but can I get out of the hallway before I tell you about them?"

I silently stood back and watched in amazement as Lily—*Lily!*—walked right into my apartment and across the living room. I closed the door before turning to look at her again.

"H-how do y-you know?" I asked, pleased that I'd managed to form a complete sentence.

"Well…," she started, dumping her stuff on my couch, "I went to go tell my crush that I had feelings for him, remember?"

I nodded.

"But it turns out my crush lied to me about living in California."

She then took a small step toward me.

"Y-you were l-l-looking for *C-Cruz?*" I asked, my astonishment ringing out of each word.

"Of course. Who'd you think I meant?"

"I th-thought you m-meant your r-r-rock star. I w-was going to open the d-door when I h-heard you l-leave, and l-let you f-find me. B-but…wh-where've you b-b-been?"

"First I was in Florida visiting my parents," she said, taking another small step in my direction. "Then I was in California, having the world's most ridiculous conversation with your extremely confused brother Mitch, who I mistook for Jake. I kept asking him about Cruz, but that's really your last name, as it turns out."

"I-I'm so s-s-sorry L-Lily," I said. "I n-never m-meant to l-lie to you."

"I know," she said. "Mitch called Jake, and he explained everything to both of us."

My heart sank.

Chapter 41

Hurdles and Hope

"E-EVERYTHING?" I asked, embarrassed now and wondering what my brother might have told her.

"Everything," she said, nodding. "Like how awesome you are. And how hard you've been working on your social anxieties on the off chance that maybe you and I could be together someday."

I could feel my face turn bright red while my eyes grew wide yet again. I studied her once more, trying to figure out where this conversation was headed, because it sure seemed like a minefield of mortification. But…well, she was still smiling. I decided I had no choice at that moment but to be brave and trust that she really was too wonderful to be cruel about my feelings for her, even if she didn't have the same sort of feelings for me.

"Th-that's t-true," I said, as my nerves caused my stuttering to accelerate. "B-but y-you don't owe m-me anything. D-don't l-let them m-make you f-feel guilty or l-like you have to d-do or s-say anything. I g-get it. W-we c-can j-just be f-friends."

"Max," she said, "I think you're misunderstanding what's happening right now."

"I a-am?" I asked.

"You are," she said, taking another step toward me. "I don't want to just be friends with you."

"You…*w-what?*"

I wondered if she could hear my heart pounding.

Suddenly, her teasing look was gone, replaced by a fire that was reflected in my own soul. It was the familiar crackling awareness that had struck us in the lobby on the very first day our eyes met, and it was back with a vengeance. The universe itself seemed to be pulling us together.

"I've already got friends," she told me. "So I'm not in the market for more. What I want is to be *with* you. To date you. To cuddle on the couch and hold your hand. To come home at the end of the day and talk with you. To know you'll be there for me and take care of me, and that you'll let me take care of you. I've loved getting to know you in our texts. You're funny and kind. You accept, encourage, and understand me. And you're brave and strong and amazing. We're friends already, yes. But Max, we're also more than that. *So* much more. Can't you feel it? Every time I see you, the pull between us gets stronger."

"L-Lily, you c-can't p-p-p-," I started. Then I trailed off, frustrated and wound up so tightly that my throat felt like it was closing. As I paused, my eyes nervously searched her face for signs of pity or exasperation. Then I realized something incredible: She wasn't trying to guess what I was attempting to say, and she wasn't nudging me to hurry it out. She was just…waiting, and without a trace of impatience on her face or in her body language. The moment felt huge to me—important and life changing. *She* was important and life changing.

Both encouraged and blown away, I tried again— "You c-can't p-possibly want to be with a g-guy who c-can't even s-s-speak," I said. Then I stopped again and studied her some more. She wasn't running, and she didn't look filled with doubts. Still…this was me I was dealing with, and I couldn't let myself believe or fully trust what was happening just yet. I worked to swat away the bubbles of hope that were starting to float and pop around me. This couldn't be real. Not a chance. She couldn't actually be into me. *Me?!*

"Let me get this straight," she finally said, breaking the silence and looking at me like I'd just suggested we fly to Mars for dinner or something. "You're standing here suggesting that I wouldn't want to be with a guy who lights me up from the inside with a simple gaze? That I wouldn't want a boyfriend who saved my life, then went full-blown superhero and chased down the guy who had my purse? I should turn my back on this superhero who, by the way, might have gotten injured doing all of that? And then he shrugged the whole thing off like it was no big deal and never even let me thank him for it because that's how caring, brave, and amazing he is? *That's* who you believe I should walk away from? Over a *stutter?* Seriously?!"

"I'm j-just th-thinking about *you* h-here," I said in my conviction that she wasn't examining the situation realistically. Dealing with me and my problems was brand new for her after all, and she couldn't possibly have thought it all the way through. "Really th-think about it. P-p-picture it. I'll embarrass you in f-front of your f-friends. You w-won't w-want to take me to p-parties or w-work events or to m-meet your f-family. I'd b-be d-dragging you into this c-cave with m-me. I-isolation is st-still isolation, even if you b-bring somebody along for c-company."

"Oh, we're not hiding anything," she said, shaking her head. "I'm *proud* of you, Max. After everything the world has thrown at you, you're still standing here with the strength and the heart of a warrior. You're still dreaming of a better life and fighting to make it happen. I want you right by my side, and anyone who doesn't like it isn't someone I want around anyway. I intend to show you off to the whole world—but only when you're ready. I know this is all new to you. We can go slow. If…wait, am I all alone here in wanting this? Don't you feel it, too?"

"Y-yeah, I f-feel it," I said, studying her face again. She looked…well, she looked like a woman who knew what she wanted. She was smart, beautiful, and strong, and she wanted the chance to be in my life. If only I'd shut up and stop throwing hurdles up between us, that is.

That's when a burst of confidence and heated longing overtook me, and I reached out my hand the way I'd wanted to do when I saw her at the elevator.

"C-come h-here," I said, smiling.

She took a slow first step, then she vaulted across the room and leaped into my arms. When I caught her, she wrapped her legs around me, and my back hit the door with the force of her momentum. She laughed at the ridiculous thudding sound while I cherished the intense sensation of holding her at last. Then she smiled back at me, softly tracing a finger down my face. And that's what did it—a flashfire quickly ignited between us, and suddenly her lips were on mine in a furious and hungry exploration. Our mouths met again and again, our lips clashing together like cymbals as her fingers worked their way through my hair. Desperation and pent-up attraction fueled our manic kisses, and I held her tighter as the moment stretched out. We were both breathless when she finally unwound herself from my waist, giving a small laugh as her feet hit the floor again.

"Wow…that was…," she said, then paused to

study my face, her arms still wrapped around my shoulders. "Nope. Can't do it. I know I'm the writer here, but I'm sorry…there simply aren't words to describe how I'm feeling right now."

"I-I've wanted to h-hold you l-like this for a l-long time," I said. "B-before you even knew I e-existed. B-but I have to s-say, being here w-with you now is b-better than I ever d-dreamed."

I brought my left hand up, and she leaned her face into it, closing her eyes. Then I brushed my thumb across her cheek gently, much the way I'd done the night of her mugging.

She opened her eyes again, and I was surprised to see the sweet moment between us disappear as a look of shock eclipsed it. I followed her gaze to see what had caused her reaction, and my eyes landed on my left arm, where the ugly scar from the knife wound snaked its way jaggedly across my skin.

"There's a lot we need to talk about," she said.

I nodded, reached out, and, for the very first time, took her hand in mine.

Chapter 42

Finally Collecting

I FOLLOWED HIM back across the living room to the couch where I'd dumped off my stuff. Yes, I could have stopped at my apartment first and tossed the bags inside. But I'd been too excited to see him and rushed right past my door without giving it a second thought.

And now here I stood with him as my heart performed acrobatics in my chest. Emotions were surging through me—and they felt a whole lot like love—for this impossibly wonderful guy who was stirring up all kinds of crazy responses in me. I glanced at him as he stopped in front of the couch. He looked uncertain about where we should sit and was likely way too polite to tell me to move my junk out of the way.

"Here, let me clear this off," I said, tugging my hand free and scooting my bags off to the side. I sat down then, thinking he'd sit by me. But after a moment of indecision, he sat on the far end of the couch sort of sideways instead, his body angled in my direction. I gave him a look of complete surprise then. After the kiss we'd just shared…

"Th-this just got a-awkward," he said, interrupting my wandering thoughts with a shrug. "I'm s-sorry. I don't even kn-know what to do. It's all n-new to me."

I kicked off my sneakers, crisscrossed my legs, and slid myself closer so we were facing each other. He reached over and took my hand again, and I watched as he gently caressed my fingers.

"But it's *not* new," I pointed out. "It's just me, your friend Lily. We've been talking with each other practically nonstop for weeks. Months, really."

"True," he said, looking back into my eyes again. "B-but I never let m-myself truly b-believe this could h-happen. I mean, I w-wanted it. I wished for it. And I've b-been w-working so hard to be worthy of it."

"Oh, Max," I said, my voice thick with emotion, "you didn't have to do a single thing. I like you, exactly as you are. I've been falling for you, you know. I instantly fell for every side of yourself that you've let me see. I feel dumb, though, for not figuring out sooner that it was one single person I had feelings for and not two."

"Th-that was my f-fault for lying to you," he said. "I'm s-so sorry."

"I know," I said. "And I get why it happened the way it did. I do. Mitch explained it to me. But I've been feeling so guilty about my attraction to you, you know, as the rock star. Don't laugh at me, but actually, my nickname for you was Soulful Guy."

He chuckled despite my warning, and I marveled at how handsome he was with such a carefree smile. And from the things that Mitch told me, I'm guessing that those smiles were probably very rare. I made a silent vow to expend plenty of energy trying to elicit as many of them as I could, then treasure each one he gave me.

"S-Soulful Guy?" he prompted.

I sighed. "Yeah. We only saw each other three times. *Three!* But you knocked me off my feet during each one. And yeah, it made me feel guilty. I mean…how could I feel those things for Soulful Guy and still have all these other feelings for Cruz? It didn't make any sense to me, and I've been so torn and unsure what to do."

"I n-needed time," he said. "B-but I'm s-sorry that put you in a w-weird place."

"I'm not," I said, squeezing his hand. "I'm grateful for all of it, because everything that happened, even the nonsense with Chad, brought us together, here, in this moment. And I think this just might be the happiest day of my life. So yeah, I'm thankful for every stupid thing that happened."

"M-mine, too. H-happiest day. B-by a mile."

"On the other side of it, one of the *worst* days of my life was when I got mugged," I said. "I was so scared for you. There was blood on my purse, and I couldn't find you even though I kept searching around our building. What happened?"

"It's n-not an exciting s-story," he said with a dismissive shrug. "I couldn't l-let him have any p-piece of you. So I ch-chased him and t-tackled him. I grabbed the p-purse and held onto his l-legs. He f-finally kicked free and l-left."

"And this?" I asked, leaning over to look at the angry-looking scar on his forearm. "He stabbed you?"

"Wh-when I was midair, he sw-swung the knife."

I closed my eyes as the many terrible possibilities fed their venom into my mind. And just as tears were starting to pool in my eyes, I felt his tender touch gently wiping them away again.

"I'm okay, L-Lily," he said. "J-Jake took me to get s-stitches. It's no b-big deal."

"It's a *very* big deal," I said. As I looked at him again, my mind attempted to capture a mental snapshot of the loving expression on his face. Then I unfolded my legs and slowly crawled toward him. He looked unsure at first, then quickly caught on and helped me get settled as I worked my way into his lap. His arms surrounded me, and I leaned my head against his chest. *Safety. Love. Acceptance.* All those feelings and more filled the air around us as I listened to the reassuring thump of his heartbeat, a sound so precious to me now. "Thank you," I whispered. "For everything."

Max's only response was a gentle tightening of his embrace.

I was finally collecting on that hug he'd promised me.

Chapter 43

Not Going Anywhere

TURNS OUT LILY LIKED being in my arms, and I liked having her there, too. I've spent a lot of time—my whole life, I guess—feeling like I didn't fit into this world. Like I'm standing outside of everything, watching through a window while people lived their lives, and wondering how to get to the other side. But lying there on the couch just then, with Lily stretched out like a cat in a sunbeam and sleeping right on top of me, I finally felt like I belonged.

Lily knew everything now. We'd finally closed the distance between us, the one that had been filled with lies and hidden identities and other secrets. She knew it all—my problems and failures and anxieties—and yet she was still here. She wasn't mad at me. She understood. And she didn't pity me, either. In fact, I think I might have actually believed her when she said she admired me and thought I'd been brave.

I'd spent a lot of time internalizing and believing only the bad stuff about myself. One glorious afternoon with her couldn't erase a lifetime of negativity, of course, but that was fine because I didn't want just one afternoon. I wanted to be with her forever.

We'd barely moved off the couch all day. It was like neither of us wanted to break the spell that was cast the moment I opened my door and found her standing there. We talked some more, ordered takeout, and laughed. I also learned about her parents and their retirement down in Florida, and she told me all about Claire and what a great friend she was. I told her more about my brothers and a little about my parents, although she knew that wasn't my favorite subject. I even told her about Wyatt Levine.

But we didn't only talk. We'd held hands and snuggled and, yeah, we'd kissed some more…

Just as I was thinking about those kisses, some sweet and some blistering in their intensity, Lily mumbled and stretched, then folded herself back on my chest. I smiled and was about to press a kiss on the top of her head when my phone lit up with a text.

Jake: So, I had an interesting conversation with Mitch.

Me: Huh. What about?

Jake: Don't play games with me little bro. What happened with your girl?

Me: I can't really answer that.

Jake: Oh no. Talk to me, Maxwell. Didn't she come see you? Wait, is she mad? She's mad about the Cruz stuff, isn't she? Let me talk to her. I'll tell her it's all my fault. That's the truth anyway.

Me: Okay. But that conversation's gonna have to wait.

Jake: Why? Aww man, I'm so sorry I messed this up for you. You think she's too mad to talk yet?

Me: Not sure. I'd ask her but she's asleep on top of me.

Jake: YOU DOG! You're messing with me?! If I wasn't so happy for you, I'd come over there and kick your butt right now.

Me: Sorry couldn't resist.

Jake: It's good, little brother?

Me: Yeah, man. Happiest day of my life. And it's all because of YOU. I can't ever thank you enough.

Jake: Just be happy, okay? That's all I've ever wanted for you.

Me: Thanks, Jake.

As I was dumping the phone back on the floor, Lily stretched again and lifted her head, her blue eyes peering up at me.

"I guess I fell asleep," she said, a guilty look on her face. "That's so lame, but I was too wired to sleep much last night. I'm sorry."

"I'm not," I said, brushing an errant hair from her face. "In f-fact, I was just t-telling J-Jake how happy I am."

"Yeah?" Her emerging smile looked darkened with worry. "I'm pretty happy, too. So happy and comfortable, in fact, that I don't ever want to leave. But I've got boring stuff like laundry and unpacking to do. Plus I've got to go back to work tomorrow."

"It's okay," I said. "Do w-whatever you n-need to do."

"Yeah, but I'm just…." As she trailed off, the smile on her face slowly wilted.

"Just?" I prompted.

"I'm just afraid this is a dream," she said finally, her words racing out in a sudden, breathless scramble. "I don't want to walk out that door, Max, I really don't. I feel like I'll wake up still wondering what happened to Soulful Guy and wishing Cruz lived closer."

"I agree it f-feels like a d-dream," I echoed as her words etched themselves onto my soul. "B-but it's real. And it's g-going to last. I mean, I c-could help you with the l-laundry if you w-want. We could keep h-hanging out. But you d-don't have to worry b-because I'm not going anywhere."

"You're...sure?" she asked, delight sparkling in her eyes now.

"Yeah, very sure. L-Lily, I'm serious about you. S-serious about *us*. You're n-not a crush to me. You're definitely not s-silly or unimportant or t-temporary. Y-you're my h-heart. It's probably s-stupid to say this so early, b-but I love you."

I watched her face closely as I said those words, pleased that they mostly came out with no trace of a stutter. They had simply appeared in the air between us, strong and ringing with the certainty I was feeling.

"I love you, too," she said, both smiling and sniffling now. "And I can't believe you'd be willing to do laundry with me."

"I've been h-hiding in here a l-long time," I told her. "You m-make me want to l-leave and do absolutely a-anything. Including l-laundry."

She tightened her arms around me and moved up to tuck her face into my neck.

I leaned over and pressed a kiss to her cheek.

"I'll love you f-forever."

Chapter 44

Abdication and Announcement

IT'S OVER. FINISHED. Gone as quickly as it appeared. What had once shaken up my life with the force of an earthquake was now nothing more than a distant memory.

That's right, I'm no longer the Queen of the Friendzone. I had to abdicate the throne once Max and I declared our feelings to each other. Nope, I'm definitely not living in *his* friendzone. I mean, yeah, we're best friends. But, according to him, I live in his soul, and my name is written on his heart. For someone who's been waging a ferocious battle against his own voice for so long, he's proven himself to be endlessly romantic and poetic.

I savor all his words, because I know exactly how precious and rare they are. For years, he saved his words only for his brother, but now he shares them with me, too. I may have seemed flighty and silly to certain people in the past, but I'm certainly smart enough to know when to treasure something so valuable. Max is my treasure, and I'm never going to take him and his love for granted. I suppose that sounds sugary and sappy, like something Tinkerbell might say while riding a unicorn. But I guess I'm okay with that.

We've been together for a few weeks now. In a lot of ways, nothing's changed. I still love my job at the dentist's office, and I'm still working on my book. In fact, Rose and Jaxon are right in the middle of longing for each other, but they're letting the things they're afraid to say to each other stand in the way of their happiness, a subject I kind of know a lot about. Don't worry, though. *Of course* they'll get their happily-ever-after—just like we did.

Max has been working a lot on his freelance web designs. He even surprised me by starting a website for when I start publishing my books. He's still going to the gym every day, too, and he's been meeting regularly with Wyatt Levine. When he comes home after their appointments, we practice the strategies he learned together. I can't tell if his speech is noticeably improving in general or if he's just so comfortable with me now that he's able to relax and talk freely, but I know he's improved. I'm so happy for him and proud of all he's accomplished. His bravery blows me away.

Speaking of bravery, tonight we're going out to dinner with Claire and Jake. It'll be the first time we've seen either of them—except when Max sees Jake at the gym—since we got together. Actually, it'll be the first time we've seen *anyone* as a couple. Claire's absolutely dying to meet him, and I know Jake's been pushing Max to meet me, too. We've been kind of putting them off about it because we're still caught up in blissed-out wonderment about finally finding each other. It all feels too fantastical and private, like something we don't want to share. But we finally gave in and set up a dinner. I think it's an important step for Max, and I know he's nervous about it. I warned him how blunt Claire could be, but that's just who she is. I hope she likes him, and I also hope he'll be able to relax around her and be himself.

Okay, I guess I'm a little nervous about it, too.

They're both so important to me, and the need to see them bond is thrumming through my veins.

Another important step is going to be telling my parents about him. I haven't done it yet, only because I was more than a little convinced that my mother would start worrying and fussing so much that they'd show up at my door within a day or two. Like I said before, Max and I have been enjoying our bubble of happiness and solitude. Having my parents stomp into the middle of it with interrogations and worries was torturous even in my imagination.

But still…I wanted to get it over with. Plopped on a park bench during my lunch break seemed like the perfect time, so I tapped their name in my contacts list before I could agonize any further.

"Liligator!" my dad boomed the moment the call connected. "How's my girl?"

"I'm great, Dad," I said, "Is Mom there? I've got news."

"Sure, honey, hang on…." I pulled the phone back from my ear, fully aware of what was about to follow. "Margaret! Lily wants to tell us something!"

I couldn't help chuckling as his voice blasted through the little speaker. He probably just gave anyone within a block of their house a jump-scare.

"Okay, you're on speakerphone," he said a moment later as my mother's voice joined in.

"Lily! What's wrong? Are you sick?"

I chuckled. "No, I'm fine, really. I just wanted to tell you that I met someone. Remember I was telling you that I had a new writing buddy?"

"Yes, of course, sweetheart," my dad replied.

"Well, his name is Max, and he's amazing…and I love him."

"Oh, Lily, no," my mom said somewhat predictably. "You can't possibly know this person well enough to trust him yet. You're a single woman, and there are all kinds of psychos out there looking to find someone sweet and innocent like you to prey on."

"Mom, for heaven's sake!" I said with a roll of my eyes. "Would you please trust me enough to figure out who I love? Trust yourselves a little, too—you know, that you raised someone smart enough to know a psycho from a good guy."

"*Of course* we trust you," my dad cut in. "Margaret, lay off her, would you?"

"We just don't know this Max person, now do we?" she said. "How am I supposed to trust my baby with him?"

"Listen, I'll either bring him down there soon or you guys can meet him next time you come to visit me," I said. "But you *will* be meeting him, because he's it for me. He's The One, Mom."

"Aww, did you hear that, Margaret?" my dad said as though she hadn't been standing next to him the entire time. "She knows it's true love. If you're sure, Lily, then we can't wait to meet him."

Oh, I was sure. There weren't any doubts or lingering questions in my mind at all. Max was strong, sweet, giving, supportive, compassionate, brave...and they were going to love him like a son the minute they met him.

When I finally got them off the phone, even after several fresh rounds of my mom's persistent protests, I was smiling.

Chapter 45

The Rest of Forever

IT WASN'T all that long ago that I was frozen—mute and immobile—on the sidewalk outside Say Java as I watched Lily's heart breaking. I felt helpless as the pain creased her beautiful face, able to do nothing more than wonder what was wrong. As she hung her head—in what I eventually learned was embarrassment and pain—I watched in silence. I couldn't help her, and I certainly couldn't comfort her. I was unseen, unnecessary, and unworthy.

At least that's how I felt at the time. And, honestly, how I'd been feeling for most of my life. It's funny how drastically life can change, though, if you're willing to take a risk and let other people help you. I did those things. I let Jake talk me into texting Lily, even though I was pretending to be Cruz. I also let him set me up with a speech therapist, and I trusted the things Wyatt Levine told me. Then I threw myself into his mindset of confidence and self-acceptance. Mitch even helped me the day Lily showed up in his world. Instead of a not-my-problem door slam, he welcomed a stranger into his home and ensured that she learned and fully understood the truth.

Yeah, I had gotten a lot of help along the way, so it turns out I wasn't alone after all. I wasn't unseen or unnecessary. Not anymore…and maybe I never had been.

"She's awesome," Jake said as soon as Lily and Claire stepped away from our table to go to the bathroom. "I love seeing how relaxed you are with her. It's like a miracle or something."

"M-miracle?" I said with a chuckle. "Ouch."

"Shut up, you know what I mean. This is exactly what I always wanted for you. How I always envisioned your life. And finally, here you are, meeting Claire and talking to her like it's no big deal. I can see that Lily's into you bigtime. It's obvious every time she looks at you. It's obvious on *your* face, too. It's a beautiful thing to witness, Maxwell."

"Yeah, things are p-pretty great," I said. "B-but what about you? You've g-got to be f-feeling like a burden got l-lifted off your shoulders, too," I said. "I've r-relied on you t-too much. And f-for way too l-long. Now you're f-finally free."

I thought he'd laugh or make a joke, or even get sappy about it. What I didn't expect was for a look of weary resignation and despair to flicker across his face, the unhappiness in his eyes suddenly glaring like lights on a billboard.

"Free, yeah," he said, his eyes turning down as he studied the drink in his hand.

"J-Jake? Wh-what is it? What's wrong?"

"Nothing. Everything's great. Really."

"I d-don't believe you. C'mon, you've been there for m-me my whole life. L-let me do the same for you. Talk to m-me. Something's on your m-mind."

"Maxwell, let this night be about you and your beautiful girl," he said. "Don't worry about me."

"You're f-freaking me out r-right now," I said, dread building in my chest now. "Are you s-sick? Is it s-something like that?"

"No, man, chill out. I'm healthy as ever. Really. I've just…okay, yeah, you're right. It's true that I've got a few things on my mind. But that's it."

"Yeah?"

"Yeah. You know, truthfully, I've been thinking about talking to you and Mitch, but…well…I can't. Not yet."

"Okay…then you'll c-come to me when you're r-ready?" I asked, something in his tone telling me to drop it and give him space. "Promise?"

"Promise," he said. "Now forget all the heavy stuff and smile, because the ladies are heading our way."

*   *   *

Later, as we walked back to the apartment building with our hands linked, I told Lily about the conversation with Jake and how it unsettled me.

"S-something big is g-going on with him," I said, the guilt gripping me tight now, "and I've b-been so wrapped up in m-my own world that I d-didn't see it before."

"Whoa—hey, give yourself a break," she replied instantly. "He probably was working hard to hide it from you. But now that the relationship between the two of you is kind of shifting…well, maybe he felt comfortable letting you see inside him in a way he couldn't before."

"I g-guess. I'm just s-sorry his life got s-swept up in my problems for so l-long."

"Yeah, well, I don't think *he's* sorry. I think he was right where he wanted to be all along."

She always knew what to say to make me feel better. Then again, she didn't really have to say a word. Simply being near her froze my worries and soothed my troubles. I squeezed her hand gently, then stopped walking. She halted then and turned back, a cute little bit of confusion dancing its way across her face.

"What's up?"

"I just w-want to take a m-moment to cherish m-my beautiful girlfriend."

"Oh really?" she said with a mischievous smile, walking into my embrace and looping her arms around my shoulders. "And just what do you plan to do with this girlfriend-cherishing moment?"

"Oh, that's an e-easy answer," I said, smiling back. "I'm g-going to stretch it out into f-forever."

She must have liked that, because her response was to reach up and capture my lips in a kiss that held the promise of a million tomorrows. I kissed her back, the pace gentle and unhurried.

We had the rest of forever, after all.

Thank You!

THANK YOU for reading Max and Lily's story! I would appreciate it so much if you took a moment to rate or review it on your favorite site.

There's more Max and Lily to come, as this is just book one in the trilogy about the Cruz brothers. If you can't wait, Jake and Mitch's stories are live now on Kindle Vella, but both will be coming soon in ebook and paperback.

<h1 style="text-align:center">Sneak Peek!</h1>

Here's an advance look at Jake's story, *The Friendship Divide: A Friends-to-Lovers Romance*. Jake has been his brother Max's helper, champion, and confidante for years. Max's well-being was his sole focus and his only priority. But now that Max has found his confidence—and the love of his life—where does that leave Jake?

CHAPTER ONE

"I'VE SEEN geriatrics with younger souls than you," Tyrone said, his headshake of disapproval at odds with the smirk that was beginning to tug on the corner of his mouth. "My grandma's got more game."

"Honestly, she probably does," I admitted. My reward for that particular honesty bomb was a snort of laughter from him, but I couldn't exactly be mad. I mean…he wasn't wrong. I was 28 years old on the outside and ready for retirement on the inside.

"Why do you even have those tattoos and muscles and pretty boy looks if you're not going to bother using them for good, my brother?" he said, leaning against the door of the training room at the gym where we both worked. "I've got a whole crowd going out tonight, including some women who would be all over you. Join us. Jake, my man, for once in your life, let your inner wild animal loose."

"I appreciate the invite, I do," I said as regret bubbled up deep inside of me where, trust me, no inner wild animal existed. In a different life, a different set of circumstances…maybe. Maybe I'd be crawling all over town every night with Tyrone and his group of friends, lighting it up with a drink in one hand and the other arm wrapped around a beautiful woman. But that had never been my life to lead, not even in college or high school. Not once. "I've got family obligations tonight."

"Family obligations," he mimicked, his tone teasing but I saw the look of annoyance flutter across his face. At some point, Ty would give up on me altogether, and these invitations would stop. They were already getting more and more infrequent. After all, I'd never once said yes. "Tell me the truth, Jakey-boy, are you in the mafia? Or wait, a motorcycle club?"

"Not those kinds of family obligations," I said with a chuckle. "Family dinner."

"Okay, grandpa, whatever you say," he said, his headshake of disapproval back in full force. "Tell the other residents at your nursing home that I said hi."

I gave a half-hearted wave as he pushed off the door jamb and headed out. As he disappeared around the corner, I worked to push back the regret that was still trying to gain traction inside me. I knew I could make it disappear if I worked hard enough, though. I was a champion at shoving back my worries and disappointments, like a human trash compactor of emotions. Everyone has their special talent. That's mine.

Acknowledgments

THIS STORY—right along with Jake and Mitch's stories—absolutely took on a life of its own inside me. It started out as a germ of an idea for something that really would have been more of a light romcom than what it turned into. I'm the opposite of Lily in that I'm a plotter, so I've got all my original plans for it still. Here's an actual excerpt from those notes (the original title I was playing with at that time was *Long-Distance Neighbors*):

Summary: She's a writer. Has lost faith in love and happy endings. She needs a beta reader. He's her neighbor and has been secretly in love with her. She totally doesn't SEE him. Somehow he finds out she needs a beta and…This part is hazy…Volunteers a "friend"? But it's really him. They start communicating via email and getting to know each other. She doesn't know it's her neighbor. Thinks he lives across the country. He gets her to start writing. He slowly realizes she's basing her hero character on HIM (the shy neighbor). She kind of confesses she thinks he's cute but…whatever…he's too shy.

Anyway, you get the idea…that was the plan. Lots of meet-cute/romcom energy. But when I started writing, it's like Max put his foot down; he wasn't happy with simply being shy. Before I knew what was happening, suddenly he had a debilitating speech issue combined with a horrific childhood, and the story just wasn't the same anymore.

It also became clear quickly that his brothers needed their own stories told. There's Jake, who put his whole life on hold to save his younger brother. What will he do now that Max is on his own two feet and doing just fine? And then there's Mitch. How long will anger, secrets, and mysteries keep him clear across the country, isolated from his brothers? Like Max, both Jake and Mitch refused to be quiet in my head until their stories were complete!

I hope you enjoyed Max and Lily's story, and I'd love to hear your thoughts about it in reviews, on social media, or via email!

As always, I'm sending out all my love and thanks to my family and friends for all their support. And a huge thank you to my friend and editor Wil Mara, who daily helps me navigate this publishing journey.

About the Author

ANNE TROWBRIDGE loves writing romances that hit major emotional beats in swoony, angsty stories in which the couples really earn their happily ever afters. Expect banter, angst, and deeply emotional connections that resonate!

She lives in New Jersey with her husband, two kids, and two dogs. When she's not reading or writing, she's teaching language arts to middle schoolers, which really should involve medals for bravery. She grew up all over the Midwest and somehow still loves to travel and see new places.

Join her and learn more about upcoming books at:

https://www.annetrowbridgebooks.com/

https://linktr.ee/annetrowbridgebooks